THE BLESSING OF BABIES

Shiloh Ridge Ranch in Three Rivers, Book 8

LIZ ISAACSON

ISBN-13: 978-1638760184

The Glover Family

W elcome to Shiloh Ridge Ranch! The Glover family is BIG, and sometimes it can be hard to keep track of everyone.

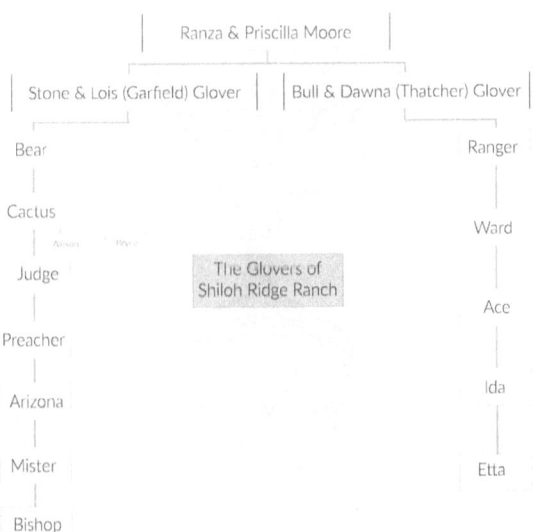

There is a more detailed graphic here, on my website. (But it has spoilers! I made it as the family started to get really big, which happens fairly quickly, actually. It has all the couples (some you won't see for many more books), as well as a lot of the children they have or will have, through about Book 9. It might be easier for you to visualize, though.)

HERE'S HOW THINGS ARE RIGHT NOW:

Lois & Stone (deceased) Glover, 7 children, in age-order: (Lois is now married to Donald Parker)

1. Bear (Sammy, wife / Lincoln (11), step-son, Stetson (2), son, Russell (newborn), son)

2. Cactus (Allison, ex-wife / Bryce, son (deceased) // Willa, wife / Mitch (12), step-son, Charlie (newborn), son)

3. Judge

4. Preacher (Charlie, wife)

5. Arizona (Duke Rhinehart, husband, living at the Rhinehart Ranch, just south of Shiloh Ridge / Shiloh (newborn), daughter)

6. Mister

7. Bishop (Montana, wife / Aurora (18), step-daughter, Robbie (newborn), son)

DAWNA & BULL (DECEASED) GLOVER, 5 CHILDREN, in age-order:

1. Ranger (Oakley, wife / Wilder (18 mo), son)
2. Ward (engaged to Dot Crockett)
3. Ace (Holly Ann, wife / Gunnison (newborn), son)
4. Etta
5. Ida (Brady Burton, husband / Johnny and Judy, (twins, newborns), son and daughter)

Bull and Stone Glover were brothers, so their children are cousins. Ranger and Bear, for example, are cousins, and each the oldest sibling in their families.

The Glovers know and interact with the Walkers of Seven Sons Ranch. There's a lot of them too! Here's a little cheat sheet for you for the Walkers.

Momma & Daddy: Penny and Gideon Walker
1. Rhett & Evelyn Walker
Son: Conrad
Triplets: Austin, Elaine, and Easton

2. Jeremiah & Whitney Walker
Son: Jonah Jeremiah (JJ)
Daughter: Clara Jean
Son: Jason

3. Liam & Callie Walker
Daughter: Denise
Daughter: Ginger

4. Tripp & Ivory Walker
Son: Oliver
Son: Isaac

5. Wyatt & Marcy Walker
Son: Warren
Son: Cole

Son: Harrison

6. SKYLER & MALLERY WALKER
Daughter: Camila

7. MICAH & SIMONE WALKER
Son: Travis (Trap)

THE GLOVERS KNOW AND INTERACT WITH THE SEVERAL of the cowboys and their families at Three Rivers Ranch too... There's a lot going on in Three Rivers!

You'll see:

1. Squire and Kelly Ackerman

Mother / Father: Heidi (owns Ackermans bakery) / Frank

Son: Finn

Daughter: Libby

Son: Michael

Son: Samuel

2. PETE AND CHELSEA MARSHALL (CHELSEA IS SQUIRE'S sister)

4 sons: Paul, Henry, John, Rich

3. REESE AND CARLY SANDERS: THEY'RE THE ADMINS FOR Courage Reins, Pete and Chelsea's equine therapy unit at Three Rivers Ranch.

Chapter One

E tta Glover pulled up to her sister's house, a police cruiser parked in the far half of the driveway. Ida's husband, Brady, worked for the Three Rivers PD, so Etta wasn't surprised to see the cop car.

Her heart did beat out a staccato rhythm, a fact she actually hated. She shouldn't be nervous to visit her twin. She and Ida had been through everything together, right from the moment of their birth.

"You will not clean her house," Etta told herself as she lifted her water bottle from the cup holder. She took a sip and replaced the bottle. "You won't comment on her clothes. Or the twins' clothes. Or anything. You're here to show her unconditional love and support. That's all. You're here to listen to her talk about whatever *she* wants to talk about. Not yourself. Not your job. Nothing about you."

Etta was trying really hard to show Ida that she wasn't jealous, as Ida had tried to keep Etta away immediately following the birth of Johnny and Judy. She knew the deepest desires of Etta's heart, and she hadn't wanted Etta to see how very hard it was to have two babies.

Etta already knew becoming a mother would be phenomenally hard. She wanted it anyway, and she didn't care if her sister had a week's worth of dishes in the sink, baby puke on her clothes, hadn't showered in days, or that the twins didn't wear matching outfits.

Ida had hated the matching outfits growing up, but Etta secretly loved them.

She got out of the car and made the trek up the front sidewalk, noting that the lawn was already starting to green, though it was only mid-January. Ida's flowerbeds waited, the earth rich and deep, and they'd planted bulbs last fall so Ida wouldn't have to do so much this spring.

She and Etta had put up a month's worth of freezer meals, but Ida had confessed that she'd only used a few. *They just aren't what I want to make*, she'd said. Etta didn't understand that, but she didn't need to understand it. She wasn't the one with a husband that worked long and odd hours, or the one trying to take care of two babies simultaneously.

Etta had learned so much in the past nine months, and one of the biggest lessons was that she didn't need to understand everything. She hadn't been able to walk down the aisle and marry Noah Johnson—a man she loved—and she still didn't fully understand that.

She only knew that she couldn't do it; that it wasn't the right thing for her, despite loving him so much. He'd loved her too, and she sent up another prayer that the Lord would bless him with happiness and anything he needed to find it.

Etta couldn't remember the last time she'd knocked or rang the doorbell at Ida's, and she didn't today either. "It's me, Ida," she called as she entered the house. The last time she'd come, both babies had been asleep in their swings, and Ida had been frantically scrubbing the couch to get something out of it.

She'd cried on Etta's shoulder for a good, long while, and Etta's whole heart had swelled with love and compassion for her sister.

Today, Ida came out of the kitchen, both twins strapped to the front of her body. She wore hope in her expression and all of her dark hair piled up on top of her head in the messiest, most elegant bun Etta had ever seen.

She grinned at her sister. "Look at you and those babies."

"This sling has literally saved my life," Ida said, returning the smile. "I can get so much more done, and they like being close to me."

"I bet they do." Etta set her purse on the floor near the side table just inside the door and went further into the house. "I'll take them if you want."

"We've just been waiting for Auntie Etta to show up, haven't we?" Ida rushed toward her and hugged Etta. The scent of lemons and soap came with her, and Etta scanned the kitchen behind her. It didn't look terrible, but it wasn't professionally cleaned either.

It was exactly how a kitchen should look that had a busy family living out of it.

Ida stepped away and started to untie the sling around her waist. "If you'll just grab Johnny," she said, and Etta reached to do just that.

"He's so big," Etta said, taking the three-week-old into her arms. "I almost brought Stetson, but Sammy says they're going to take him to cut his hair today when they pick up Lincoln from school."

"His first haircut," Ida said, smiling fondly. "I don't think these two will do that for a while. Poor Judy is still bald as a billiard ball." She laughed lightly as she removed the sleeping baby girl from the sling. "Go sit down, Etta. I know you want them both."

Etta did what she said, because she did want both babies on her lap. She sighed as she sat down, though she'd been driving for thirty minutes in a seated position. She shifted Johnny to her right side, and Ida settled Judy on her left.

She grinned down at the babies, both of whom remained asleep. "You must've worn them out this morning already." She beamed over to Ida, who'd sank into the recliner, her legs tucked underneath her.

"I took them to get their pictures done," she said. "Whitney Wilde has this whole studio over on the east side of town, in the cutest little farmhouse. You would love it, Etta."

"Yeah? Does she just shoot there?"

"She does all of her wedding photography there. Her newborns can be outside or inside, and we did some in both areas. She's got these antique milk cans with wheat coming out of them, and tons of cowboy props."

"Sounds amazing," Etta said. "Did you do cowboy pictures?"

"No, I talked to Whitney several times, and we wanted something a little more classic." Ida continued to talk about the photos, and how they'd taken a duo shot with Brady's police hat.

"I can't wait to see them," Etta said as Johnny grunted and groaned, pulling his tiny little legs up into his body. She tucked him closer and wobbled her elbow to bounce him back to sleep. He yawned, and that was the cutest little action Etta had ever seen.

Her heart melted, and a longing sigh came out of her mouth.

"Tell me what's new with you," Ida said, and Etta looked up.

"When do you take the babies in again?" she asked instead. "I can come help you."

Ida blinked at her, her smile faltering. Etta wished she could pull the offer back inside her mouth, but she'd also learned not to try to cover up a blunder with more words. So she remained silent too.

"You don't have to—I want to know about you too," Ida said. "I literally can't talk about the babies all day, every day." She reached up and released her hair from the pretty bun. "It's all anyone wants to know about. *How's Judy eating now? Is Johnny still hogging all of your milk?*" She shook her head and looked up at the ceiling.

Etta knew that tell, and that look meant Ida was trying to get her tears to go back inside her eyes.

"I don't want to talk about the babies. You're my best

friend and my sister. Tell me something that has nothing to do with a pregnancy, a baby, a sister-in-law, a brother, a cousin, or anything at the ranch."

Etta's mind raced. "That's my whole life, Ida."

"No, it's not," she said firmly. "We've always had more to our lives than family and that ranch."

"I live there now," Etta said. "I don't think I'm as separated as I used to be." She shrugged and snuggled Judy closer too. "I don't hate it. I get to bring Stetson down to my suite some nights, and it's nice to not be alone in the room."

Ida gave her a soft smile. "Remember when you told me you couldn't wait to graduate so you could finally have a bedroom of your own?"

Etta's smile popped onto her face. "You're kind of a slob, Ida."

"And you're so proper and prim," she shot back.

"I'm trying to loosen up," she said, the one thing she hadn't told anyone yet coming to her mind.

Marshall Redmond.

"In fact, I'm getting so loose that I'm going to meet a man for a date that I met on Cowboy Connection."

Ida opened her mouth to respond, then only sucked in breath. "What?" exploded out of her mouth as she exhaled. Her eyes rounded and held only shock. "You're using Cowboy Connection?" Ida actually leaned forward. "Didn't you say you wouldn't be—and I quote—caught dead with that app on your phone? That it was too kitschy with that alliterative name?"

Ida's expression harbored delight now, and Etta held

her head high and rolled her eyes as if this conversation was ridiculous. "I'm aware of what I said."

"Where's your phone?" Ida got to her feet, searching the couch near Etta, and then the end table.

"Don't you dare look at my phone," Etta said as Ida made a dash for Etta's purse by the door. "Ida." She tried to get up, but two tiny humans severely restricted her.

A cry of triumph filled the air, and Etta heaved a great sigh of frustration. It was too late; Ida had the phone, and only an act of God would stop her from looking at it now.

"Listen," Etta said. "It's a dating app, okay? You're supposed to flirt on it. You say things you wouldn't normally."

"I can't wait to see what you said," Ida said, plenty of glee in her tone.

"Ida," Etta pleaded, and that got her twin to slow down and stop. Their eyes met, and Etta could see the moment Ida came back to reality. She lowered the phone to her lap. "Tell me about him."

Relief filled Etta. Ida had always respected Etta's privacy, and she knew her better than anyone else on the planet. "You have to promise not to let your eyes get all big like they just did."

"I won't," Ida promised.

"And I don't want you to interrupt me a thousand times." Etta glanced down at her niece and nephew. "No questions until the end. And if you ever find yourself starting a sentence with 'you should' or 'you should have,' stop. Instantly."

Ida made a crisscrossing motion over her heart and nodded soberly. "You got it."

Etta took a moment to decide if she needed any more rules for Ida. Satisfied, she said, "I started talking to him on Christmas. He's got a nice profile picture, with a big, black cowboy hat. So I tapped on the heart. He responded within five seconds, and we've been talking here and there."

"Can I call a lie when I hear it?" Ida asked.

"Is that a question?" Etta fired back.

"I'm just saying that you just lied," Ida said, settling back into the recliner and folding her arms. Etta noted that she still had the phone secured in her hand.

"Fine," Etta said. "We chat quite a lot these days."

"Every day," Ida said.

"Yes, every day. Happy now?"

"Multiple times?"

"You're asking questions."

"They're valid questions."

"Yes, multiple times. He's up early because he's got a small farm on the highway going toward Amarillo. I'm up early because I can't sleep. So we talk in the morning. I usually send him a little picture of what I've made for lunch."

Embarrassment flooded Etta, though she did love to cook, and she loved to make her dishes prettier than they tasted.

Ida's eyes sparkled like blue diamonds. "So exciting."

"He responds to that, and usually asks me a couple of

questions about what I like to eat, what's the worst thing I've ever cooked, my favorite candy, that kind of thing."

"So he's not just some creep. He's trying to get to know you."

"Seems that way," Etta said. "So it's been a few weeks, and he asked me if I'd like to go to dinner this weekend, and I said yes." She lifted her chin again, feeling the need to defend herself. "We're going casual. Pizza and salad at The Pepperoni Garden."

Ida squealed, and Etta realized she should've made that a rule. No squealing. "I haven't even been out with him yet," she said. "He could show up and be twenty years younger than he said he was. He could have six kids I don't know about."

"You love kids."

"I don't want six from the moment I say I-do," Etta argued.

"Would you date a single dad?" Ida asked, in classic Ida style.

Etta had the thought to tell her that she'd said no questions, but she didn't really mind it. "I'd date a single dad, yes," she said. Noah had children. She didn't mind a man who came with kids. She wanted a man who wanted *her* kids.

"I really just want someone with a good heart. Someone who loves Texas, loves God, and can put up with literally twenty-five people at family dinners."

"Someone who can make you a mom," Ida added quietly.

Etta took a breath. "Who knows if that will even

happen?" she asked, vocalizing the thought that had been plaguing her for months. "I mean, look at Oakley and Ranger. They want kids so badly. More than me, even. And they have such a hard time getting pregnant."

Judy squirmed, her face scrunching up as she started to cry. Etta's focus shifted, and Ida got up and took Johnny. That way, Etta could focus on the fussy little girl.

"She needs to be fed," Ida said. "Then she'll sleep for a little bit, and we can talk about your outfit and what you're going to do with your hair on Friday."

Relief hit Etta again, because she did need help with her clothes and hair. "I don't want to come across as too stuffy."

"I won't let you," Ida promised as she moved into the kitchen.

Etta got up and followed her, and together, they made a bottle each for the baby in their arms. "Don't think I don't know that you gave me the pukey baby," Etta said, hipping her sister as she took Judy back into the living room.

"I don't have a clean shirt in the whole house," Ida said, following her. "I can't afford for her to throw up on this one."

Etta giggled and gave the bottle to Judy. "Here you go, baby. You're such a good girl, aren't you? You aren't going to puke on the bestest aunt in the world, are you? No. No, you're not."

"Oh, she is," Ida assured her. "Count on it."

Etta smiled at the little girl, because she was perfection, with Ida's nose and a tiny little chin the shape of all the Glovers she'd have to grow into. "Ida?" she asked, looking up.

Ida looked up from her son. "Hmm?"

"I don't want a word about me using the app or going out with Marshall at the luncheon."

"Cross my heart and hope to die," Ida said, repeating something they'd said as little girls. Etta grinned at her, and they both went back to taking care of the baby in their arms.

Etta had held onto her relationship with Noah Johnson too, and she couldn't help thinking that maybe she *should* tell all the ranch ladies about Marshall. She'd have gone out with him by the time they met next week.

Willa was hosting the luncheon this month out at the Edge Cabin, and it would be easy for Etta to tell them all on the group text they shared only with each other. Her brothers and male cousins wouldn't need to know.

They wouldn't care anyway, Etta thought. She'd considered telling Cactus, who was the best of anyone at keeping secrets. He also had great advice, and Etta had grown closer to him since she'd left Noah standing at the altar by himself, her entire family staring him in the face.

In the end, Etta decided she'd keep Marshall a secret for just a little longer. She wanted to meet him first, and she didn't need the pressure of eight people asking her how the date had gone before it had even ended.

That decided, Etta went back to her duties of bestest aunt, a title she took seriously and would be working to maintain for years to come.

Chapter Two

✿

Willa Glover added another squirt of mustard to the potato salad, knowing that Holly Ann wouldn't like it. She didn't like mustard in general, though she acknowledged its presence in some dishes.

For her, she preferred the more vinegar-based potato salads, while Willa much preferred all the mayo and mustard she could get.

"It's your luncheon," she told herself, the house so quiet without everyone there. Her husband took his dogs out onto the ranch with him, and Willa could admit she missed Galaxy and Tank when they weren't in the house. They adored Cactus, as most living things did, but Tank would cuddle with Willa while they watched movies in the evening.

Mitch, her son, took Frost to school with him. He needed the hearing dog, and the two of them were inseparable.

That left Willa at home alone, though she had a couple of ranch dogs she could probably open the back door and call for. Cactus kept horses in the barn about fifty yards behind the house too, but Willa was in no shape to ride them right now.

Her second baby—her first with Cactus—was due in only eight days.

She put one hand on her bulging belly, ready for this little boy to make his appearance. "Not until after the luncheon, okay?" she whispered to her son.

After her accident, she hadn't dared to dream she could have the life she currently lived. Happily married, in a beautiful, new home, with her son, a doting, caring husband, a new baby on the way, and the ability to stand up and teach the gospel of Christ once a month.

Even if she did have to deal with all the dogs.

Willa smiled to herself and took a moment to thank the Lord for all of her blessings. She'd come so far since that day she'd been texting and wrecked her car. So much had changed, including the very core of who Willa was and who she wanted to be.

She covered the potato salad and slid it into the fridge. The hot ham sandwiches she was serving were set to go into the oven, and she took out the tray and set it on the counter. They were best if they went into the oven at room temperature, and she had a few minutes before they'd be ready.

She went through the motions of straightening the pillows on the couch. Cactus said she had a pillow problem, and that he knew a good therapist who could help.

She'd quipped back that if buying too many pillows was her worst problem, he should be thanking God every morning and every night.

They'd laughed, and Willa prayed again that nothing would be wrong with their son. She had no idea if Cactus would even be able to survive if anything was wrong, and Willa hated the way the unknown made her so uneasy.

As she got out the cleaning bucket and wiped down the guest bathroom that sat off the front door, she thought about the tests and scans she and Cactus had done during her pregnancy.

The doctors couldn't find anything wrong with the baby. Nothing in his heart. Nothing in any of his organs. Nothing in his limbs. Nothing.

Willa knew he could still be deaf, as there was no way to tell that from an ultrasound.

She just wanted the infant to be born, because then she and Cactus could stop worrying.

Of course, parents never stopped worrying about their children, as Willa knew all too well, having lived without Mitch in her immediate life for a couple of years.

Her thoughts wandered to his father, and if he'd ever want to be back in Mitch's life. She didn't know what she'd do then, as Mitch was now thirteen years old and had plenty of opinions of his own.

They didn't talk about his father, and Willa had the distinct feeling that she should.

"Hello," Oakley called, and Willa stepped out of the bathroom to greet her.

"Hey, there." Willa beamed at the other woman—her

sister-in-law. Or cousin-in-law. Something. Cactus and Ranger, Oakley's husband, were cousins.

All of the women who'd married into the Glover family felt like sisters to Willa, and she embraced Oakley easily. "How's Wilder?"

"Good," Oakley said with a sigh. "He's cutting more teeth, and I swear there's slobber on everything I own." She gave Willa a smile though, and they went into the kitchen together.

"Ranger's keeping all the kids today," she said. "Doing some work on Two Cents while the others go out onto the ranch."

"That's brave of him," Willa said. "Three boys under the age of two will keep him busy."

Oakley smiled and went right over to the oven to preheat it. "I hope so. We're hoping to have another one before Wilder is two."

She'd told Willa that before, but Willa didn't want to ask how it was going. Oakley would share with the family when she was pregnant. It had taken her and Ranger a few tries last time, but they both wanted more than one child.

Cactus wanted a big family too, and Willa hoped she'd be able to provide the children they both desired. She'd be thirty-eight this year, and with the injuries she'd sustained in her car accident, this pregnancy had not been easy.

Worth it, she thought. But not easy.

The back door opened, and Charlie stepped inside. She scanned Willa and Oakley in the blink of an eye and said, "Oh, good, I'm not the first one here."

She wore a pair of tight jeans and a blue sweater that

brought out the azure in her eyes. Her hair flowed over her shoulders in waves, and she was petite and thin and about the exact opposite of Willa.

Just wait until Holly Ann gets here, she thought as she smiled at Charlie. She hugged her, noting the other woman held her tightly. "You're welcome here anytime," she said. "First or not."

"I know." Charlie grinned at her as she stepped back. "I was hoping to talk to you two for a minute." She wore nerves in her expression, and Willa had talked with many anxious people in her life as a pastor.

"We've got time," Oakley said, also giving Charlie a hug. "What's up?"

"Okay, uh." She glanced at Willa and then back to Oakley, who picked up the cutting board and set it on the counter in front of her.

"I don't want the Glovers to invest in Below Zero, and I don't know how to tell them." Her hands went round and round each other, and along with the wide eyes, told of her nerves.

"Have they said they are?" Oakley asked. "For sure?" She turned to get the apples and pears Willa had bought.

She'd already made the fruit dip out of cream cheese, crushed pineapple, and caramel, and it chilled in the fridge. Oakley would simply cut the fruit they'd eat as everyone arrived.

"No," Charlie said. "I don't want to waste their time. Preacher says they're meeting tomorrow, and I feel like I need to get it off the table so they can talk about something else to invest in."

"Why don't you want them to invest in Below Zero?" Willa asked, watching the other woman. She did love everyone up here at Shiloh Ridge, but she definitely had closer relationships with Oakley and Charlie specifically. Cactus's sister, Arizona, was a close friend too.

"I'm not even sure I'm going to keep it open," Charlie said. "With my broadcasts, and the chemistry demos, and if Preacher and I start a family.... It feels like too much."

Oakley and Willa exchanged a glance, but neither of them asked Charlie if she was pregnant. She and Preacher had gotten married less than a month ago, almost on a whim, when they'd been stranded up at the ranch during a wind and ice storm that had caused a landslide.

"So the ice cream shop is below the broadcasting and the demos?"

"I think so?" Charlie guessed, sighing after speaking. "I don't know. I just know I don't want to be responsible for their money."

"Just tell Preacher that," Willa said. "I'm sure he'll understand."

"Yeah," Oakley said. "He's really diplomatic in the meetings. He won't make it a big deal with the others."

Charlie nodded. "Okay. Yeah, okay." She sighed again, almost like she needed to exhale out all the worries about this. "How are you, Willa? I didn't think you could get bigger, but I think you did."

"Right?" Willa looked down at herself, hating that she couldn't see her feet. "I'm hanging in there."

Someone knocked on the back door, and it opened a

moment later. "I'm here," Lois said, and Willa stepped over to hug her too.

"Oh, my dear." Lois held her tightly. "You're so beautiful." She beamed at Willa, and then did the same to Charlie. "How's the newest Glover?"

"Good, ma'am," Charlie said, still a little formal with Lois despite coming to a few luncheons now.

"Getting along okay now that you can't get rid of Preacher?" Lois asked, her dark blue eyes sparkling.

"So far so good," Charlie said with a smile and a light laugh. "I just go in the office and close the door. It has a lock."

The others laughed, Willa included. She got out the fruit dip and put it beside the board where Oakley was arranging the pears and apples.

Sammy, Montana, and Holly Ann arrived at the same time, already engaged in what felt like an important conversation. They shrugged off jackets and tossed them over the back of the couch nearest the front door.

Greetings went around, and Willa marveled at the strength of the women in the room with her. She loved hosting the luncheons, though she only got to do it once a year.

"What would you do?" Sammy turned to everyone. Listen to this and tell us." She started detailing the situation with her parents, who were really getting too old to live on their own—at least if they had to keep taking care of the big house they owned in town, and the acre it sat on.

"They don't want to lose their independence," Sammy said. "But Bear can't keep going down there every other day to help them." She sat at the bar and reached for a pear. "I feel like I need to sit down with them and have a hard conversation I don't want to have."

Everyone looked at Willa, and she realized a lot of them turned to her for advice like this. Number one, her parents were past this stage of their life. They lived in an assisted-living facility already and had for a few years now.

"Well," she said slowly as the oven beeped. "Those kinds of conversations aren't fun, but they do need to happen. I'd start by asking them what they want their life to be. Yard work? Constantly asking for help? Hiring out certain tasks like mowing the lawn and shoveling the snow when it does come? Or something else."

"You're kind," Lois said. "Just see how they're feeling."

"They've got two houses on that property," Sammy said. "They could sell them and make a lot."

"Especially in the Three Rivers housing market right now," Holly Ann said. "My dad sold his place for way more than he thought he could."

"It's a seller's market," Montana said. "Has been for a while. I couldn't afford a house even a couple of years ago. That's why I was living with my aunt and uncle."

"How are they?" Willa asked. "I haven't seen them for a while."

"Good," Montana said with a smile. "We're actually thinking of naming our son Robert."

"Oh, I love Robert," Sammy said. "I was thinking of that when someone said Russell. We went with that instead."

Willa loved listening to the ladies talk, and since she'd given her opinion, the spotlight was off her.

She slid the tray of ham sandwiches into the oven and turned back to the group just as the front door opened again. Etta entered first and turned back as she said, "Hey, everyone."

She held the door for her mother and Ida, who had both twins strapped to her body. The arrival of the babies —now just shy of a month old—caused a huge uproar.

Willa hung back, as did Oakley and Charlie, and the trio watched as Sammy and Lois claimed the babies and sat down on the couch to mother them.

Etta got her mother settled on the couch between them, and then the twins came into the kitchen too.

"Thanks for having us, Willa," Ida said, tears in her eyes. "It's the first time I've left the house with both babies, and it's so much work." She grabbed onto Willa and hugged her tightly. "Y'all should be glad you didn't marry a cop."

"Why's that?" Oakley asked, taking her turn to hug Ida hello. She had a special relationship with the twins, because she'd married their oldest brother. Oakley didn't have any family in the area, and her relationships with the women in her life meant a lot to her.

Willa could relate. She just had her brother in town, and while she'd once spent a lot of time with him—he'd done everything for her when they'd first moved to Three Rivers together—she hadn't seen Patrick as much since marrying Cactus and moving to Shiloh Ridge.

"Are we ready?" Etta asked, returning to the kitchen

with a chocolate cake in each hand. She placed them on the counter and pushed them back out of the way.

"Arizona isn't here," Willa said. "The food won't be done for a few minutes either. But there's fruit and dip."

Since Etta had moved into the homestead, Willa saw her often. If she didn't eat lunch at the homestead with everyone, Willa almost always made something here at the Edge Cabin.

Sometimes Charlie came. Sometimes Oakley did. Most often, Etta arrived with Cactus, and the three of them enjoyed a meal together. They didn't even have to talk for it to be calming and comfortable.

"What about Dot?" Oakley asked, looking at Willa. "Did we invite her?"

As if summoned by their names, the back door opened, and Zona and Dot entered. The last woman in glanced around as if she didn't belong, and Willa prayed she'd find a spot in the family.

She would, Willa was sure. She just wasn't sure where that was right now.

She wore Ward's diamond ring, so she'd be joining the crew up here at the ranch soon enough. Since Cactus and Ward were both second sons, they were quite good friends. Willa and Cactus had hosted Dot and Ward for dinner just a couple of nights ago.

"Hi, Willa," Dot said, and Willa hugged her close.

"Hey, Dot. How are you?"

"I feel like I can't breathe."

"Join the club," Charlie said.

Willa started to laugh, really laugh from her belly,

which wasn't all that comfortable with the baby pressing against everything.

"I'm not wrong," Charlie said, leaning against the far counter, where Dot joined her.

They watched the chaos of Zona's arrival, and she ended up with one of Ida's babies while Willa pulled out the potato salad and Oakley started opening bags of chips.

"All right," Willa said a few minutes later. "All right, everyone. We're ready to start." The women stopped chatting, and Willa beamed around at them. "I'm so grateful to have you all in my home and in my life." Her lungs seized when she tried to breathe, and she hoped she could blame her emotions on her pregnancy. "We've decided the host of these monthly luncheons has to share something the others might not know about her, and mine is pretty easy."

She gestured to the spread on the countertop. "One of my favorite foods is potatoes. I don't think I've ever met one I didn't like. Fried, roasted, baked, mashed. If you can do it to a potato, I like it."

A few of the ladies twittered, and Willa did like the institution of sharing something about herself that no one knew.

"So I made my favorite version of potato salad. It's my mother's recipe, and it probably has way too much mustard for Holly Ann."

She grinned and waved her hand like she didn't mind. She was so nice, she probably didn't.

"And potato chips. My favorite are these sour cream and cheddar, but I like them in all their varieties. Then I made the hot ham sandwiches on potato rolls, because if you can make a potato into flour and then bread, I'm all-in on that."

She laughed, glad when the others did too. "Etta brought the chocolate cake, so thank her for that, and Oakley made all the fruit. Let's pray, and these sandwiches will be done." Willa checked the timer on the oven, and if one of them could pray for a solid two minutes, she'd like to hear it.

"Lois is hosting next month," Willa said. "So that means she prays this month."

Lois handed the baby in her arms to Dawna and stood, glancing around at everyone with an expression of love on her face.

Willa knew exactly how she felt, as her heart felt extra full today for some reason. Maybe the Lord was simply expanding it to make room for more people to fit inside, and Willa pushed against her worries and fears about her unborn child, knowing she'd love him no matter what.

A WEEK LATER, WILLA WOKE IN THE MIDDLE OF THE night. "Cactus," she groaned.

Her husband didn't move in the bed beside her. He'd assisted in the delivery of three calves yesterday, with the first one coming at three a.m.

Willa groaned, the sound hardly human as she sat up, all of the muscles in her midsection tightening past the point of comfortable. They kept going, and she cried out.

As she achieved a sitting position, she panted through the pain. "Cactus," she said again.

Still nothing.

She reached for the lamp on the bedside table and snapped it on. "Charles," she practically yelled.

"I'm right here," he said, and Willa looked right toward the doorway. He entered the bedroom. "It's time." He didn't ask, and he didn't wait for her to confirm that she was in labor. There must be something on her face that said it all.

"The bag's in the car," he said, reaching her in a few long strides and putting his hand on her elbow to help her stand. "Let's go."

"I'm not dressed," she said, barely able to take a step. "Neither are you."

Cactus looked like he'd argue, then he said, "Okay, let's put some pants on you." He turned and grabbed the stretchy, black pants she'd been wearing exclusively for the past few days. He steadied her as she stepped into them.

He moved away from her and stepped out of his cotton shorts and into a pair of jeans while she pulled her night-gown over her head and replaced it with the same baggy sweatshirt she'd worn yesterday.

"What about Mitch?" she asked, taking Cactus's arm again. "Oakley said she'd come, but it's the middle of the night."

"It's four-thirty," Cactus said. "What about Charlie?"

"I'll call her right now." Willa remembered her phone. "I left my phone on the nightstand."

He stood her next to the doorway. "Lean on this. I'll get

it." He jogged back and grabbed it, then proceeded to help her to the car. She called Charlie as he ran toward the driver's seat.

"You're in labor," Charlie said instead of hello. "I'm on my way. Preacher and I will take care of Mitch until you come home."

"How are you awake?"

"Preach went out at three-thirty," Charlie said. "They've got another mother who was laying down in the fields." She blew out her breath. "Don't worry, Willa. I'll get Mitch to school easy peasy. Then I'm sure I'll see you at the hospital."

"I'm sure you will." Willa sighed as the call ended. "Is there any way to not tell anyone?"

"Sure," Cactus said. "You call Charlie back and tell her not to tell anyone, and we don't either." He glanced at her, the bumps in the road making her back ache. "Is that what you want?"

"Yes," she whispered.

"Make the call."

Willa did, another contraction coming as they rumbled along. She breathed through it, surprised when another one came before they'd reached the epicenter of the ranch. "They're coming fast," she said.

She had two more before they reached the highway, and she'd gotten smart enough to time them. "They're only three minutes apart," she said.

By the time they arrived at the hospital, thirty minutes later, Willa was having a contraction every two minutes. They rushed her into a delivery room, and the lights were so bright. The voices so loud. Didn't they know it was five o'clock in the morning?

"Ready to have this baby?" Dr. Specter asked, and Willa wondered when he'd arrived. Her first delivery had been so much scarier, though a river of anxiety flowed through her now too.

"Yes," she said at the same time Cactus did. If there was someone more nervous than her, it was him. He wore his nerves like clothes, and Willa found herself wanting to comfort him. Another contraction tore through her, so she couldn't.

Things moved quickly, and the next thing Willa knew, Dr. Specter told her to push. "Right now, Willa."

She did as he asked, Cactus standing right behind her, supporting her. After several minutes, the doctor laughed and said, "Here he is."

Relief rushed through Willa, though she wasn't finished yet. She still relaxed back into Cactus, both of them breathing hard.

Two nurses rushed toward the bed, and that was when Willa noticed how deathly silent the baby was.

"He's not crying," she said, tears filling her eyes. "Cactus, why isn't the baby crying?"

Chapter Three

S ammy stared at her phone for an extra beat before she leapt from the settee where she'd been tying her shoes. "Bear," she called, rushing out into the living room. "Bear!"

"Downstairs," he bellowed, and Sammy kept running, though she needed to get her two little boys before she could leave the house.

"Cactus and Willa had the baby," she said, arriving at the top of the steps. "We have to get to the hospital right now." Anxiety and love rushed through her. Cactus had been a solid foundation for her in a tumultuous time, and she loved him like he was her own brother.

"They did?" Bear appeared at the bottom of the steps and started up there. "He texted you?"

"It's on the family string," she said. "They must've been there for hours already." She hurried back into their suite, her mind rushing over what she needed to do in order to be ready to go. "They didn't text the moment they left, which makes me so mad."

"I'll help with Stetson," he said.

"I can feed Russell on the way down in the car," she said. In the boys' room, she reached for the fussy baby while Bear moved over to the toddler bed to wake Stetson. Sammy hated waking either child, because they were so much like their father when they got woken up.

Beasts.

Grizzly bears.

She smiled at Russell, who had quieted with her touch. "They didn't text the moment they left," she repeated, her mind catching up to the situation. She looked over to Bear, who had the miniature version of himself folded over his shoulder. "Maybe they don't want us there."

Bear's phone rang, and he shifted Stetson to one arm and tugged his phone from his pocket. "It's Cactus now." He tapped and had to do it again to get the call connected. "Hey, brother. Just saw your text."

"Put it on speaker," Sammy said, moving over to her husband. "I want to hear."

"It's okay, Cactus," Bear said, pacing away from Sammy, his frown deepening.

"What is it?" Sammy asked, her heartbeat booming through her whole body. Her stomach dropped out of her body, and she hadn't felt like this since the day she'd found out her sister had died. "Bear."

She followed him as he said, "We're on the way. I'll tell everyone." He hung up and spun back to Sammy. "The baby wasn't crying, and the nurses whisked him away before Willa or Cactus could see him." He reached up with his free hand and hugged Stetson close to him.

Sammy hated the unrest in her husband's soul. He wanted everything to be perfect for everyone, and Bear sometimes thought if he willed such a thing, it would come true.

It didn't always.

"Let's go," she said, tucking Russell further into her arms. "I'll grab the diaper bag, and we can buy food for Stetson down there."

"I have to talk to Ranger," Bear said, following her as she practically ran out of the bedroom. His voice sounded like he'd sucked in helium, and Sammy realized for maybe the first time that Cactus wasn't the only one who'd gone through some grief after his first son had died. Sometimes watching someone go through a terrible experience could be just as hard as living it oneself.

"I can't believe he didn't text us the moment they left for the hospital," Sammy said, her own tears mixing with her fury. "If he had, we'd all be there to support him right now."

"Exactly," Bear said. "We'd all be there."

Sammy headed straight for the front door while Bear detoured into the kitchen. She slid into the back seat of the king cab truck and started to nurse Russell. Bear came out a few moments later and strapped a now-awake Stetson in his seat while Lincoln climbed into the front seat where Sammy usually rode.

"Ma," he said, smiling at her. "Toes."

"Who gave you that toast, buddy?" She grinned back at

her first-born son as he tried to get the slice of toast in his mouth. He missed at least half the time when aiming his food toward his mouth, but he managed to take a bite.

"Link, do you have your backpack?"

"Dad said I didn't have to go today." Link turned and looked at her.

"Sorry," Bear said, buckling his seat belt and starting the truck.

"It's okay," Sammy said. She couldn't even think about school right now. "Just get us there fast, Bear." She couldn't even imagine what Charles was going through. Alone in the hospital, without his baby.

Please, Lord, she begged, closing her eyes against the hot tears gathering there. *If there is any way possible—any way— please preserve the life of that baby and make him perfect and whole.*

Charles had wanted children for so long, and just when he'd thought he'd gotten it all, his first son had been born with a congenital heart condition. He'd died after only four days of life. Charles's first marriage had dissolved, and he'd retreated to the Edge, where he'd lived for almost a decade in isolation.

Sammy had a strong bond with Bear's brother. She suspected it came from losing someone so near and dear to her soul. When Heather had died, Sammy's entire life had changed. For a long time, she hadn't known how to live in a world without her sister. In a world where she was the only remaining child.

Once she'd met and married Bear, she'd learned how much she wanted a big family. They were doing everything they could to make it so, but she had limits, and Bear was already forty-seven years old.

With his late start on marriage and family, they'd been talking about what was reasonable for them. She was far younger than Bear, but she didn't want to raise children by herself. She religiously made him go to the doctor for his annual physicals and cancer checks, because his father had been dead by this age.

She switched Russell to the other side as Link started talking about the upcoming science fair. She wasn't looking forward to that, but she hoped Heather would be proud of how Sammy was raising her boy. He loved Bear with his whole heart, and they'd asked him over Christmas if he'd like to be adopted by Bear.

Lincoln had burst into tears and asked if such a thing could really happen. They'd assured him it really could, and Bear and Sammy had started learning what they needed to do in order to make Lincoln their legal son. She had custody of him, but being a legal guardian wasn't the same as being his mother.

Bear pulled up to the hospital and said, "You guys get out here. Leave me Stetson. We'll be right behind you."

"Okay," she said. She slid from the truck and waited for Link to climb down. "Thanks, Bear. I love you."

"Love you too."

She faced the hospital, her body vibrating with nervousness. "Come on, Link." She entered, holding her head high and her shoulders straight. The blanket she'd used to cover herself and Russell hung down, and she hitched it higher as she searched for the way to the maternity wing.

"This way." She strode down the right hall and had to tell herself not to run when she saw the department up ahead. A man stood at the nurse's station, and she knew exactly who those shoulders belonged to. "Charles," she called, trying to keep the panic from her voice.

She failed, and Cactus turned.

He held a baby in his arms, the bright blue blanket practically sending life signals into the air. "Go give Uncle Cactus a big hug," she told Link, and the boy ran ahead of her.

Cactus grinned, then laughed, then crouched down when Link arrived. He'd grown so tall over the course of the last year, and he'd spent almost every day last summer with Mitch and Cactus on the ranch. Then every day after school too.

Lincoln adored Cactus, as did most children.

He tipped the baby toward Link, and the infant started to wail. It was the most beautiful sound in the world.

"Don't you *ever* do that to me again," Sammy said as she arrived, her voice breaking on the last word. She swept right into Cactus's space as he stood, their two babies between them. She couldn't hold back the tears any longer, and she cried right into his chest.

Just as quickly as she'd done that, she stepped back and swatted at his shoulder. "It's way too far to the hospital from the ranch when the news is bad."

"I'm sorry," he said quietly. "Willa and I just wanted a few minutes with him alone." He gazed down at the quieting baby in his arms. "We just got him back about ten minutes ago."

"And?" Sammy asked, looking at the baby. He sure seemed perfect to her, with a shock of dark hair on his head that seemed to glow a bit auburn in the harsh hospital lights.

"He's perfect," Cactus said, his voice breaking. "He was just plugged up, and they were worried about his temperature. So they took him to an incubator and cleaned him up."

"Can we switch?" Sammy asked, her voice pitching up again. "I'm sure everyone else is on their way, and then I'll lose him to your mother." She sobbed but pulled the sound back quickly.

Cactus met her eye, and the bond they'd always shared strengthened and grew. "I'm sorry I didn't call you. I'd prayed so hard that everything would be perfect that I didn't believe it would be anything but that."

"It was perfect, Charles," she said, starting to move her month-old baby to hand him to Link. "He is perfect. Link, take your brother." She passed Russell to Lincoln and then took Cactus's baby from him. "What did you name him?"

"Willa wants to name him Charles."

Sammy looked up from the perfectly pink face of the sleeping infant. "You don't?"

"I...don't know." He took Russell from Lincoln and smiled at the boy. "He's gotten so fat since I saw him last."

Sammy giggled and looked back at her new nephew. "He likes to eat, that one."

"Cactus," Bear called, and Sammy turned toward him.

He carried Stetson in his right arm, the boy smiling as if it was his duty to make sure everyone who met him that day knew how bright the world could be.

"Brother," Cactus said, stepping around Sammy and going to greet his brother. They embraced, and Bear said something to Cactus that Sammy couldn't hear. She didn't need to hear it. Just seeing them and the love they had for one another after everything they'd been through in the past couple of years was enough to make her heart whole.

LATER THAT MORNING, SHE STOOD AND TOOK RUSSELL from Zona. "I'm going to take these monsters home." She'd like to stay longer, as she'd only seen Willa for a few minutes. She'd looked good, with a glow about her that spoke of her love for her son. She was willing to share him with everyone in the family too, and Sammy knew how hard that was.

"I'll go with you," Oakley said from the nearby couch. "We can talk about the birthday party."

"Perfect." Sammy grinned at her and searched for Bear. He stood out of the way, talking with Ward and Preacher. Doing business, as always. She approached and said, "Baby, I need to take the boys home. Russell needs a nap, and Oakley and I are going to work on the boys' birthday party."

"Sure," he said. "I've got work to do too."

"I can drive," Sammy said. "You can stay and come back

with Ranger or someone. I'm sure there will be a spare seat."

"Are you sure?"

"Yep." Bear wouldn't want to leave, not yet. He loved hanging around the hospital and holding the new baby, bringing food to the new parents, and ensuring they had everything they needed. "I just need the keys."

He fished them from his jacket pocket and handed them to her. "I'll make Ranger drive by the bakery," he said. "Get us a pecan pie and one of those cherry pies."

"You always know exactly what I need, cowboy." She stretched up and kissed him. A cry behind her only reinforced her decision to leave, and she broke the kiss and turned back toward the waiting room.

Stetson's wail had silenced, but both Charlie and Holly Ann were reaching for him. He'd obviously fallen, and if they weren't careful, he'd burst their eardrums once he found his breath and could scream again.

"I'll get him," Bear said. "You go—" The last of his sentence got drowned out by the ear-splitting wail of their son.

———

"Okay." Sammy exhaled as she collapsed into a chair at the huge picnic-style table in the homestead. "They're both asleep."

"Let's listen for a minute," Oakley said with a smile. She closed her eyes and tilted her head slightly. "All three babies are asleep." She whispered the last sentence.

Sammy basked in the silence of the homestead too. *Quiet* and *the Glovers* didn't really go in the same sentence, and the homestead was the hub of family life on the ranch. "Everyone is at the hospital," she whispered.

"No one's going to come in singing at the top of their lungs."

"No one is going to be here to eat lunch."

Oakley opened her eyes and giggled. Sammy laughed with her, but her heart did something strange inside her chest.

She hadn't planned to talk to anyone about the plans she and Bear had been discussing, not until they were final and they were ready to make the announcement together. "Oak," she said, and her very best friend in the whole world looked up from her birthday party list.

Tears filled Sammy's eyes.

"What is it?" Oakley asked, abandoning the plans they'd been making for their sons' dual birthday smash. It was happening in March—only about six weeks from now —as both Stetson and Wilder had been born in that month. Wilder would turn one, and Stetson would be two.

"Bear and I—we've...."

Oakley waited patiently, as this wasn't the first serious talk the two had shared. Sammy wasn't great with telling others how she felt, but many looked to her as the leader of the wives group because she'd married the oldest Glover first.

"We're thinking about building a house of our own," she said. "Not because we don't love living here with you and Ranger. It's not that at all. Okay? You have to know it's not that." She brushed at the tears in her eyes.

"Of course I know that," Oakley said quietly. She looked down at the papers in front of her, a tactic Sammy had seen many times before. Oakley just needed a moment to think, to explore how she felt about what she'd just learned.

"If I can," Sammy said. "I'm going to keep having babies close together until we have four. Maybe five." She couldn't believe she'd just said that out loud, but she had. "Bear wants five, but I keep telling him it's a lot of work to grow a human inside my body."

Oakley gave a half-laugh and half-sob. "I'll miss you so much."

"It'll be right here on the ranch, of course," she said. "We're thinking out by Cactus, because he's got that small farm anyway, and we won't lose any farmland."

"Out on the Edge?" Oakley raised her eyes to Sammy's. "That's so far."

"It's not that bad," Sammy said. "And you can come out there every day and find some peace and quiet."

"Not with five kids under the age of five," she said, smiling through the emotion in her eyes.

Sammy burst out laughing then, because she couldn't argue with that. She leaned toward Oakley and hugged her. "I love you so much, Oak. I'll always love you like my sister."

"And I love you the same," Oakley whispered. When they parted, she inhaled deeply and wiped her eyes. "I suppose it will be nice to have more bedrooms for my own family."

Sammy's eyebrows went up. "Yeah? Are you...?"

Oakley shook her head, some of the darkness re-entering her expression. "No, not yet. But if I even have one more baby, our suite will be too small. The conference room is a permanent part of our place."

"True," Sammy said. "We haven't told anyone else, obviously. The house isn't even started yet."

"Have you talked to Bishop?"

Sammy shook her head. "He won't have time to work on it. Not with Montana due so soon, plus all the work they're doing at Zona's and then down at the Kinder Ranch."

"Bear hired Micah Walker again."

"Bear hired Micah Walker again, yes," Sammy said. "Bishop and Montana don't know, and we'll want to talk to them privately too."

"I'll keep it between Ranger and I," Oakley promised, and Sammy believed her when she made promises.

"Okay." She took a big breath. "Those boys won't give us much time. Let's see what we can get done for this birthday party before they wake up."

Chapter Four

Oakley set the pregnancy test on the vanity and pressed her eyes closed to pray. It wouldn't change the result of the test—the hormones were already there or they weren't—but she wasn't praying to be pregnant.

"Help me accept Thy will," she said. That was all. She was working on accepting God's will instead of begging for her own desires, and it was dang hard work. She reminded herself of all the many blessings He'd already given her, including an adoring husband, brilliant friends, and the little boy she could hear babbling down the hall from the bathroom where Oakley had barricaded herself.

Ranger had been using their master bathroom, but Oakley couldn't stand to wait for another day to take the test. She was seven days late now, and she needed to know.

She didn't feel sick, but then, she'd barely been ill during her last pregnancy.

She stood and looked down at the test, but it was still

processing. She left it sitting on the counter when Wilder yelled, something he'd been doing more and more often when he was ready for her to come get him from his crib.

"Mama's coming," she told the boy once she'd opened the door and entered the hallway. She opened Wilder's door, which sat right across from the bathroom, and found the boy standing up in his crib. He began to bounce when he saw her, his baby brown eyes brightening and his little legs propelling him up as his chubby fingers gripped the top rung of the crib.

"Good morning, buddy," she said, lifting him from the crib with a giggle. She loved this time of morning with her son, because he was so happy and so soft and so beautiful.

"Morning, my family," Ranger said, entering the room too. "Did I take too long in the bathroom?" He swept his arm around Oakley's waist and pressed a kiss to her temple.

She leaned into his touch. "Mm."

"Let's go get breakfast today," he said. "I'll bet they'll make the pancakes heart-shaped at the diner."

"Twist my arm," Oakley said, tilting her head back to look at him. She smiled and accepted his kiss. "I'd love some heart-shaped pancakes. Did you get my Valentine's Day gift? I left it on your nightstand."

"No," he said. "I must've missed it."

"Well, go get it," she said, her attention wandering across the hall to the bathroom. She followed him to the doorway and waited until he'd entered their bedroom. "There's something in the guest bathroom I want you to check too, please."

"All right," Ranger called back. "It better not be that toilet. I fixed the leak."

Yes, he had. Oakley looked through the open doorway and saw the pregnancy test there. She wasn't close enough to read the lines.

She turned away with Wilder, saying, "Daddy's taking us to breakfast for Valentine's Day. Let's get you changed and dressed, bud."

She began to get the job done, Ranger's voice exclaiming about the oatmeal carmelitas he'd just found on his nightstand. "I love these," he called.

He could really thank his sister for those, but Oakley was going to take all the credit. Ranger's love language consisted of being in the know with what Oakley felt and thought and food. She hadn't told him she was late yet, but he'd know soon enough.

"Thank you, babe," he said as he came back down the hall. "I can just have these for breakfast."

"Nope," she said, reaching for a fresh diaper. "You mentioned breakfast, and now that's what I want."

He chuckled and wrapped her up in his arms. "I love you, Oakley. With everything I have."

"I know you do," she said, enjoying the warmth and strength of his arms around her. "Wilder's going to wear his heartbreaker sweater today. Aren't you, bud?"

"I'll go check that gol-darn toilet," Ranger said. "If we need to get a couple of parts or something while we're in town, we can."

Oakley said nothing, because her stomach felt so tight,

like she'd swallowed her voice and it had filled her to the brim.

Ranger already had his boots on, and she focused on the clunking of them as he crossed the hall and entered the bathroom. His footsteps stalled, and Oakley pressed her eyes closed.

Help me to accept Thy will.

"Oakley," he called. His footsteps returned at double the clip, and he appeared in the doorway of the nursery once more, the pregnancy test in his hand and pure light shining from his eyes.

Tears filled hers, because she already knew what the test said. Ranger's face said it all.

He still said, "You're pregnant," and she quickly set Wilder in his crib wearing only a diaper so she could go hug her husband.

He cradled her face in his hands and gazed at her. "This is the best Valentine's Day present ever."

"I love you, Ranger Glover," she whispered.

"I love you too." He kissed her again, and Oakley had often lost herself to the cowboy touch, the gentle stroke of his mouth, and the absolute way she could feel his love for her. Today, she did the same, all while their first child babbled in the crib behind them.

She finally pulled away and tucked herself into his arms. "I'm going to call the doctor after breakfast," she said. "I might need to do those progesterone shots again. Then...." She let the word hang there while she drew a deep breath.

"Then?" Ranger prompted.

"Then I think I'd like to call my mother," she said. "Tell

her the news and ask her if she'd like to come when I have the baby this time."

Ranger shuffled backward and looked at her, clear shock in his expression. "Really?"

"Really," Oakley said. "It's okay, Range."

"But what if she says no?"

Oakley had to accept that such a thing could happen. Her mother hadn't attended her wedding, nor had she come for Wilder's birth. Of course, Oakley hadn't told her about the baby until after Wilder had been born. She wanted the decision to belong solely to her mother this time.

"We've been talking more and more," Oakley said, aware her voice had pitched up and that she was actually defending her mom. "I want to tell her, and perhaps she can be more involved this time."

"If you feel right about it," he said. "I'll support you in whatever happens."

She nodded and traced her fingers down the side of his face. "I hope it's another boy and has more of the Glover genes this time." She turned back to Wilder, who definitely looked more like her than Ranger. Since they were both dark-haired, he'd gotten that too. His curled the way Oakley's did, and he was a gorgeous baby with all that dark, curly hair and his long eyelashes.

He didn't have a stitch of the Glover blue eyes in his, and Oakley could only see the shape of her nose, her chin, and her eyes when she looked at her son.

"I hope it's a girl and she looks just like you," Ranger said, winding his arm around her waist again. "If you get his clothes out, I'll finish getting him dressed while you get ready."

She wasn't going to pass that up, and she quickly pulled out the clothes she'd been saving for Wilder to wear on Valentine's Day. She hurried through changing out of her pajamas and into real clothes, pulling her hair back into a ponytail, and then studying the pregnancy test for a few moments.

Ranger had left and taken Wilder downstairs, and Oakley could take as much time as she wanted. She peered at the two pink lines, an increased measure of joy and hope and gratitude filling her. She pressed her eyes closed and dropped the test into the trash can. Then she collected her phone from the top of the dresser where she'd set it and texted her mother.

"How many people did Bear invite?" Oakley asked as the barn came into view. Cars and trucks filled the gravel lot in front of it, sending a twinge of emotion through her. She wasn't feeling particularly like partying tonight, but Ranger's hand in hers tightened.

"Everyone at the neighboring ranches," he said. "The Walkers. The Rhineharts. The Bellamores."

"Mister will be happy about that."

"He told Bear he wouldn't come if Libby did. Bear told him to make his own choices, based on what he felt like he needed to do."

"I like Libby."

"Yes, well, Mister does too."

As they drew closer, bright red hearts started to rotate and shine on the outside of True Blue, bringing a smile to Oakley's face.

"That's festive," Ranger said, a smile in his voice. He carried Wilder in his arms, and she stepped to hold the door for him so they could enter. Music met her ears, along with the sweet smell of candy and something salty. She sincerely hoped it was caramel popcorn, as Lois had promised to make a batch of her Texas-famous treat that Oakley had been known to eat by the fistful.

They went through the lobby together and rounded the corner to face the hall. The disco ball had been brought out, and it threw silver squares all over the room. A few people were dancing already, but most loitered near the tables that had been set up in front of the kitchen serving window.

Holly Ann and Charlie worked over there, putting out platters and dishes. People carried small plates in their hands, some with miniature cupcakes and tarts on them. Some had tiny finger sandwiches and clusters of two or three grapes.

"There better be bigger sandwiches than that," Ranger grumbled.

"You ate a week's worth of food at breakfast," Oakley teased.

"Hey," he said. "We're eating for two now."

"*I'm* eating for two," she said, grinning up at him. They laughed, and she added, "You will dance with me tonight, right, cowboy?"

"Of course," he said. "Right after we eat."

"Da, dad, da," Wilder said, bouncing in Ranger's arms.

"That's right, bud," Ranger said. "Time to eat." He entered the hall first, and Oakley followed him. She picked up a couple of roast beef sliders—much bigger than the finger sandwiches, which she bypassed completely. She took a kebab with a cherry tomato, a ball of mozzarella, and a cube of basil gelée. She'd eaten these at Holly Ann's before, and she picked up another one, knowing she'd want it.

After she'd filled her plate, she moved to stand at a chest-high table with Montana and Bishop. "Have you two been here long?"

"Aurora wanted to come first thing," Montana said, indicating the dance floor where her daughter swayed with her boyfriend, Oliver Walker. "I'm dead on my feet already."

"I would be too," Oakley said. "I'm surprised you're here."

"My bathtub is calling my name pretty loudly," Montana said with a smile.

"How's Zona's house coming?" Oakley asked, picking up one of her roast beef sliders.

"Slow," Montana said with a sigh. "I'm afraid we won't finish it in time."

"Yes, we will," Bishop said. "Don't worry about it, baby. It's a house."

"I promised her it would be done before I had the baby."

"And we will." Bishop pressed a kiss to his wife's cheek. "Ace just walked in, and I need to talk to him."

"Okay," Montana said, and her husband eased away from her. Ace had arrived with Preacher and Judge, and Oakley watched with Montana as Mister also entered the barn. He paused right in the doorway, already scanning the space.

Oakley did the same, and she found Libby standing on the opposite side of the barn, to Mister's left and near the front of the barn where the altars always stood for weddings.

They seemed to know precisely when the other was near, as Libby turned her head from the conversation she was having with her sister and looked directly at Mister.

He spotted her too, ducked his head instantly, and went right. He swiped his cowboy hat from his head as he went, and Oakley watched as he made a hard right turn and disappeared down the hall that led to the changing rooms.

"I wish I could help them," Montana said.

"It honestly sounds like it's a mess between them," Oakley said. "Not that I know everything."

"Bishop says the same thing," Montana said, reaching up to run her hands through her shockingly blonde hair. "I really am going to go home and take a bath."

"Want me to walk with you?" Oakley asked. "It's dark tonight. No moon."

"No, you stay and eat more of those Caprese kabobs." Montana grinned at her, and Oakley smiled right on back. She didn't want to stay at the party for long either, and she could easily use Wilder as a reason why she had to leave early.

Ranger wouldn't want to stay either, as the man hadn't been able to break his dawn wake-up habit even though he didn't always go out on the ranch like he once had.

"Can I have this dance?" a man asked, and Mister stood there.

"Of course," Oakley said, leaving her now-empty plate on the table in front of her. She took his hand and let him lead her out onto the floor. The romantic song piping through the barn made Oakley smile, and she casually put her hand on Mister's shoulder.

"Are you going to ask Libby to dance tonight?" she asked.

"Do you think I should?" He didn't glance in Libby's direction.

"I don't know, Mister. I don't really know what's gone on between you."

"I don't either," he said. "That's the problem." He sighed and shook his head. "She's my best friend. Or she was, once. I went out there and apologized after what happened at Christmas. We've texted a little."

"So maybe just ask her to dance," Oakley said. "It can be casual, like this."

He nodded and didn't say anything else. Oakley let him have his silence and his space, and when the dance ended, she hugged him. "Be brave, Mister. It'll work out."

"Thanks, Oakley." He didn't go ask Libby to dance the next song, but he got food. Libby edged away from her sister and danced with one of her brothers. Then one of the teenagers from the Rhinehart family.

Mister danced with Charlie, and then his mother. Watching the two of them literally dance around each other made Oakley want to march over there and mash them together. "Dance and be nice about it," she'd tell them.

"Ready to go?" Ranger asked, coming to her side.

"Mm, no," she said. "I have to see if Mister and Libby are going to dance together." She glanced at her husband. "Where's Wilder?"

"Etta has him," he said. "She's going to keep him in her suite tonight." Ranger ran his hand down Oakley's side and leaned closer. "I thought we could use a night to ourselves to...celebrate."

"Mm, I like the sound of that," she said, leaning into her husband's kiss. Still, her eyes never left Mister as he kissed his mother's cheek and turned toward Libby Bellamore. "Oh, here he goes."

A squeal started to build inside Oakley, and as Mister paused in front of Libby, clearly asked her to dance, and she nodded, Oakley let it out.

"Finally," Holly Ann said, and Oakley looked over to Charlie and Dot, who were actually clapping. Willa and Cactus hadn't come tonight, though they'd sent Mitch over to hang out with Lincoln and Bear's family.

Oakley sighed as Mister finally took Libby into his arms—and they didn't dance in the easy, casual way Oakley had danced with him, with his one hand on her waist, and the other holding hers out to the side.

Oh, no. Mister put both hands on Libby's waist and drew her right into his chest. He leaned down and whispered something, and Oakley could feel the magic of a fun, exciting relationship with a sexy, smart man permeating the air with them as the origin point.

"Okay," she said with a sigh as she tucked her hand into Ranger's. "I'm ready to go home now."

Chapter Five

Holly Ann Glover pulled up to her sister's farmhouse and smiled at the red, white, and pink hearts still hanging in the windows. Valentine's Day had come and gone a week or so ago. Holly Ann should know, as she'd been counting the days until February twenty-fourth, the day she was due with her first baby.

She parked her truck—the one her husband Ace had bought her for her birthday last summer—and sat in the cab. She wanted to visit Bethany Rose, because she loved her only sibling with the force of gravity. The heat of the sun. More than anyone else in the world besides her husband.

Things had been difficult between them over the past several months. Bethany Rose had never said anything, but Holly Ann had eyes and intuition, and she knew her pregnancy hurt her sister. She wished it didn't. She'd prayed that Bethany Rose would feel only love and acceptance from her. She'd begged God to give Bethany Rose a baby of her own.

She and her husband Kevin had been trying for a lot longer than Holly Ann and Ace had, and sometimes Holly Ann's guilt kept her up at the ranch where she lived instead of coming here, to her sister's small farm on the north side of Three Rivers.

They still got together for lunch every single month, but at least three of the last nine months had been strained and short.

Holly Ann picked up her phone and turned off the ignition. She'd probably have her baby in the next couple of days, God willing, and she didn't want any animosity or tension between her and Bethany Rose. She wanted her sister at the hospital, and she wanted her sister to be one of the first people to hold her new baby.

"Bethany Rose wants that too," she told herself as she went up the wide, wooden steps to the front porch that spanned the entire width of the house. Holly Ann loved this farmhouse, and she paused and looked up into the white-painted rafters of the porch.

She knocked and opened the door almost in tandem, calling, "Hey, Bethy. It's just me."

The scent of marinara sauce met her nose, as did a rush of warmer air. Happy to be out of the wind, Holly Ann stepped inside and closed the door behind her quickly.

"Heya, Holly Ann," Bethany Rose said, turning from the stove, which sat against the back wall of the farmhouse. A gaping living room, a dining set, and an island separated the two sisters, and Holly Ann started the trek through the house, her back protesting so much movement.

Holly Ann had stopped doing much around the house a couple of weeks ago, and she hadn't catered an event since the beginning of the year. She'd been bored for several days, and then she'd figured out how to entertain herself around the ranch.

There were plenty of opportunities to explore nature at Shiloh Ridge. She could feed chickens and turkeys, go horseback riding—though she hadn't in her advanced pregnancy—walk a dog or five, and visit any number of people.

She spent a lot of time with Montana, as Ace and Bishop were best friends. Their houses were practically across the street from each other, though technically, Holly Ann had an entire meadow to herself. No other houses could be seen from anywhere in the house, and to get to her front porch, one had to drive down a tree-lined lane for about twenty-five feet.

"I'm starving, and something smells amazing," Holly Ann said with a smile, watching her sister for a sign for how today would go.

Bethany Ann wiped her eyes and turned back to the stove.

Holly Ann's steps slowed, and she made a big show of groaning as she sat on the barstool at the island. She could bring up something else. Ask about the farm. Find out how Kevin's calving season had gone. He and Bethany Ann owned this farm together, and they worked it together. They had no other cowboys or cowgirls to help, and the single-man operation wasn't very big. But it was profitable, and they loved each other and the land.

"What's wrong?" she asked instead.

"Nothing," Bethany Rose said, but her voice rode up an entire octave.

Holly Ann got up, glad her height made her baby weight more distributed than Willa's and Montana's was. Arizona was taller too, and while she and Holly Ann had definitely gotten bigger, they didn't look as uncomfortable as the others.

She rounded the island and approached her sister. "I brought you a birthday gift."

Bethany Rose sniffled, and Holly Ann put her arm around her. "Talk to me, honey. What's wrong?"

Bethany Rose turned into Holly Ann's arms, a sob wrenching its way from her throat. "I'm fine. Really."

"You're crying." Holly Ann didn't want to suggest that her sister's tears were because of Holly Ann's baby. Panic struck her that perhaps her sister wouldn't be able to mentally and emotionally come to the hospital.

Bethany Rose pulled away from Holly Ann, but kept a grip on her shoulders. Her lighter brown eyes searched Holly Ann's dark ones, and Holly Ann saw mischief there. "What's going on?" she asked.

"I'm pregnant," Bethany Rose said, immediately bursting into tears again. "I've wanted to tell you for so long, but I've been so scared about losing another baby." She turned back to the stove and stirred the sauce bubbling there. "I've been to the doctor like, five times, and they've been monitoring everything. I'm fourteen weeks now, and Doctor Xavier says he doesn't think there's any danger of miscarriage at this point." She sniffled and wiped her eyes on her sleeve. "So Kevin and I decided to tell people, and you're the first one who knows."

Holly Ann's smile could not be contained on her face. It grew and grew and grew, as did her joy. "Oh, I'm so happy for you." She leaned her head against Bethany Rose's shoulder and looked at the meal her sister was putting together.

The moment between them only solidified that they'd be sisters and best friends forever, no matter what happened. "I'm so sorry these past few months have been stressful for you," Holly Ann whispered.

"It's not your fault," Bethany Rose whispered back. "Life sometimes doesn't deal a fair hand."

"That it does not."

"I've been so happy for you and Ace too, Hols. You know that, right? Even if I've acted a little jealous sometimes?"

"Of course I know that." Holly Ann stepped away from her sister and reached for the plates. "You'll come to the hospital when I have the baby, right? I want you there. Kevin too, if he can get away from the farm."

"I'll be there," Bethany Rose said. She drew in a deep breath. "Okay, I made eggplant parmesan, and this is Grandma's homemade marinara. I know it won't be as good as yours, but I tried."

"It smells wonderful." Holly Ann hated being a chef as much as she loved it. No one could simply put a meal in front of her without some comment about how it wouldn't be as good as what she made. Such comments annoyed her, though she'd never said anything to anyone.

Bethany Rose bent to open the oven, and she pulled out two perfectly cooked slabs of eggplant. She poured the spaghetti into the sauce, mixed it all together, and served them each a plate with pasta and eggplant.

They sat at the table, where Bethany Rose had put a salad sometime before Holly Ann had arrived. The conversation was easy, and they did talk about the farm, about the ranch, and about their husbands.

"How's the new house?" Bethany Rose asked. "Kevin and I would love to come after you have the baby. I can come and stay with you even." She wore a look of hope on her face, and Holly Ann couldn't deny her.

"That would be great," she said, going back for another bite of spaghetti. "Did you...are you going to tell Mom about your baby?" Holly Ann looked up and caught her sister's eyes dropping back to her plate.

"Did you?"

"Yes," Holly Ann said. "She congratulated me and went right back to her own life." Holly Ann couldn't pretend that her mother's reaction didn't hurt. It did hurt. It hurt badly, but Holly Ann had had about seven months to come to terms with it.

Their mother had left them behind years ago, and her reaction to Holly Ann's marriage and subsequent pregnancy had only solidified that she really had no interest in the people she'd cut from her life.

"You could tell her," Holly Ann said, her voice softening. "But don't expect anything, Bethy. She won't come. She probably won't send a gift. Nothing."

"Then why bother?" Bethany Rose asked. "I'll just tell Daddy. He'll be excited."

"Daddy will be ecstatic," Holly Ann said with a smile. "He texts me every morning, every afternoon, and every night, just to find out if I'm having any labor pains." She laughed lightly, because where Holly Ann had lost her mother all those years ago, her father had stepped in and taken over the role of both parents.

"Have you been to his house lately?" Bethany Rose asked, already shaking her head.

"Not in a while," Holly Ann admitted. "Why? What's he doing now?" Her father loved to people-watch. As a former detective, he swore he could tell more about people he'd never met than people who knew them well.

"He's doing that thing where he writes down every license plate of every car that goes by his house."

"Why?" Holly Ann asked. "He's got that great community now. Why doesn't he go do, I don't know, the sixty-five-plus exercise class?"

"Can you imagine?" Bethany Rose giggled. "He'd take over the class about halfway through. That poor instructor."

Holly Ann laughed with her sister. "He's not that bad."

"Hols, yes he is. He stood up in the HOA meeting and said he could do a better job than the president."

"Well, they *did* remove that guy," Holly Ann said, grinning at her sister. She'd only eaten half of her food, but she couldn't stuff in another bite. She groaned as she stood.

"This was so good, Bethany Rose. Really. I'm just so big, and I can't eat very much."

"I gave us a lot too," she said. "It's fine. Just throw it away. I made a ton so Kevin could have some tonight."

Holly Ann cleaned up after herself and even started boxing up the leftovers for Bethany Rose's husband. Dull pain pulled through her back, but Holly Ann ignored it. Her body had been talking to her like that for a week now, never happy when she did much more than walk from the couch to the bathroom.

"Did you want your gift now?" she asked.

"Yes, please," Bethany Rose said, clapping her hands. She wore the light of a small child on Christmas Day in her eyes, and Holly Ann loved that she was always so enthusiastic about presents.

"It's not much," Holly Ann said. "Don't get excited." She returned to her purse and dug inside it for the small ring box.

The bag fell to the ground, and Holly Ann peered at it for a moment. Bending over was so much work, and Bethany Rose's chair scraped the tile as she stood. "I can get it."

"I got it." Holly Ann bent for the strap of her purse, and white-hot pain lanced through her back now. She froze as a cry came from her mouth.

"Holly Ann." Bethany Rose rushed forward, her hands grabbing onto Holly Ann's forearm. "Are you okay?"

Holly Ann met her sister's eye, pain and panic pouring through her. She managed to shake her head. "My back," she said. "I can't even stand up straight." She put both hands on her back and pressed there, trying to get her body to cooperate with her.

Something popped, and Holly Ann wasn't sure what it was. Nothing seemed out of the ordinary in Bethany Rose's kitchen, and something warm and wet started to permeate Holly Ann's awareness.

"Oh, no," she said, looking down at her belly. She couldn't see past that, but she had the distinct feeling like she was wetting her pants.

"What?" Bethany Rose asked. "Holly Ann, what?"

She tried to hold everything in, and the wet sensation continued. She pulled in a breath and turned toward the stove. "Two-fifteen," she said. "I think my water just broke." She reached for Bethany Rose. "Help me to the bathroom, would you, Bethy? And bring my purse. I have some pads in there."

Her sister flew into motion, swooping in to get the fallen purse and then assist Holly Ann down the hall to the bathroom.

"Your pants are wet," she said.

"Can you tell if it's colored?" Holly Ann asked, her mind working overtime. "I need to call Ace."

"Shouldn't we go to the hospital?" Bethany Ann knelt in front of Holly Ann as she sat on the toilet.

"Yes," Holly Ann said. "He'll have to meet us." She fumbled for her phone amidst all the other junk she carried in her purse. "Does it smell?"

"No smell," Bethany Rose said. "It just looks like your jeans are wet."

"It's not staining them?"

"No," Bethany Rose's voice trembled. "Is that good or bad?'

"It's good." Holly Ann finally found her phone and jabbed at the pinned name at the top to call her husband. "Baby," she said when he answered. "I think my water broke. I'm with Bethany Rose, and she's going to take me to the hospital."

Her back pulled at her again, causing her to groan. "I think I'm having contractions in my back."

"Are you sick?" Ace asked. "To your stomach? Cramping there?"

"Not really," Holly Ann said. "Should I call before I go?'

"No, baby," he said. "Go. I'm on my way back to the house, and I'll be there soon. Remember they said if your water breaks you have to deliver the baby within twenty-four hours? You should just have your sister take you."

Tears filled Holly Ann's eyes, but they weren't from sadness or fear. "I love you, Ace," she said. "We're going to have a baby."

"Yes, we are," he said, his breathing coming quicker. "I'm on my way, love. Don't have him without me, okay?"

"Because I'm in so much control of that," Holly Ann joked. "I don't have the baby bag, Ace. It's in the kitchen by the garage door."

"I'll get it."

Holly Ann nodded though he couldn't see her. "See you soon." She handed the phone to Bethany Rose, because she honestly couldn't even think about what to do with it now that the conversation was over.

A ripple moved across her stomach, and she said, "You

have to drive me to the hospital, Bethany Rose. I think I just had a contraction. What time is it?"

"Two-twenty-two," Bethany Rose said, rising to her feet. "Let's go. I'll call Daddy on the way."

Holly Ann nodded, quick little bursts of her head. "Let's go."

HOLLY ANN SUCKED IN A BREATH AS ANOTHER contraction started. "Again," she said.

"Again?" the nurse asked, turning from her clipboard. She glanced from it to Holly Ann to the monitor. "Yep, again. They're every forty-five seconds now."

Holly Ann felt like she'd been in the hospital for days, but it had probably been an hour. Maybe more. Maybe less. Bethany Rose stood at her side, and while Holly Ann was grateful beyond measure to not be alone, she wanted her husband there.

She pressed her eyes closed against the discomfort, trying to remember to breathe. When she didn't, once the contraction ended, she was left light-headed with a pounding ache in the back of her skull.

"Can you go call Ace again?" she begged her sister. "And how long does it take for that epidural to kick in?"

"Ten more minutes, and you should feel nothing," the nurse assured her. "Just pressure."

The pressure was enough to make Holly Ann's vision spark white. "Will I make it ten more minutes?"

"Maybe," the nurse said, and she seemed utterly

nonplussed. Holly Ann wanted to lunge out of bed and grab her by the shoulders. This was important. This was her first child. She needed answers, and not in a flippant tone.

The door opened, and Ace walked in. Finally.

"Holly Ann," he said, running the last few steps to her.

She burst into tears and reached for him, the level of relief that he'd arrived more than she'd ever experienced before. "They're coming so fast now," she said, crying against his shoulder. "They hurt so much."

"It's okay," he assured her. "It's fine, love. I'm here, and we've practiced, and you're going to be so amazing at this." He nodded at Bethany Rose on the other side of the bed.

"I'm gonna go, Hols," she said. She leaned over and pressed a kiss to Holly Ann's cheek. "Ace will bring me the baby as soon as he can."

"That I will," he promised her, and Bethany Rose left.

The nurse did too, and Holly Ann panicked. "Where is she going? I need her here."

"Holly Ann," Ace said, and she looked at him wildly.

"We need her here, Ace. Go get her back."

"Look at me, hon. You're in a complete spin." He put his hand under her chin and held her very still. "Right here, Holly Ann." He smiled at her. "There you are. Breathe in with me."

She did, some measure of calmness coming over her. "And out," his melodic voice said.

She released her breath and focused on the love of her life.

"Okay," he said. "We don't need that nurse. They know

what they're doing here. We're ready for this, and you'll know exactly what to do."

Another wave of pain rolled through her, and Holly Ann said, "Here's another contraction." She groaned and ground her teeth together. "Look at the clock on that monitor," she said. "The nurse will need to know it."

Ace did what she said, and a few minutes—and five contractions—later, a whole team of people came into the room, including Dr. Robison. He smiled at Holly Ann and Ace, looked at the printout from the monitor and said, "It's time to meet your son."

The baby came only minutes later, wailing as he arrived. Holly Ann cried out of love, relief, and gratitude. Some because of the pain, sweat, and labor she'd been through.

"Here he is," Dr. Robison said, putting the baby right on Holly Ann's chest. "Wipe him all down, Momma. Daddy, do you want to come cut the cord?"

Ace pressed a kiss to Holly Ann's head, took a moment to look at their son, and then he went to stand beside the doctor. Holly Ann could barely see her son through her tears, but she managed to catch a glimpse of him.

Everything became so clear then. All the chaos in the room disappeared, and it was just her and her baby, mother and son, in that single moment together. Oh, how she loved him.

"I love you," she whispered to the tiny human as she lovingly wiped his face with the blanket she'd been given. The baby opened his mouth and cried, and Holly Ann laughed and wept at the same time.

"What are you going to name him?" the nurse asked, and Holly Ann couldn't look away from the infant.

"Gunnison Bull Glover," she said, reaching with both hands to pick him up. She wrapped him in the blanket and marveled that something so small had felt so large inside her body. "Come on now, baby Gun. Time to eat."

Chapter Six

Dorothy Crockett pressed her fingers together, really seating the leather gloves on her hands back into place. She didn't mind the hard, physical labor her job sometimes required, and she bent to pick up another paver.

She'd come to Shiloh Ridge Ranch alone today, because she'd be staying for dinner and then wedding preparations after that. She hadn't seen her fiancé yet, but he'd come by soon enough. Ward always did. He was kind, attentive, and loving—all attributes Dot would not have assigned to the man a year ago.

She set the hexagonal paver in the spot where it belonged and turned to get another one. Life on this ranch sure did feel tinged with magic, and she couldn't wait to experience it fully. The other ranch wives had incorporated her into their fold, and she'd truly enjoyed the luncheon she'd attended last month.

She didn't know where she fit yet. She could barely remember all of their names. They all seemed to have ranch living figured out, and they all seemed to want as many kids as the Glover men could give them.

Dot wasn't so sure about that. She and Ward had spoken briefly of children, and it was definitely a conversation she'd like to revisit. Her closest friend among all the women was Charlie Perkins—now a Glover, Dot supposed. She too didn't seem enamored with the idea of preserving peaches and popping out babies every nine months.

"You're not being fair," Dot told herself and the wide Texas sky above as she took a break and reached for her water bottle. Just because six of the Glover family women had had babies recently or would have a baby in the next few months didn't mean they'd all be straight onto the next one.

Every single one of them had a different personality, and Dot had liked talking to Zona at the January luncheon. Lois, Ward's aunt, was also especially kind and welcoming. Willa was as well, and Dot had been out to the Edge Cabin twice since the birth of Willa's baby.

Willa never made anyone feel like their choices were the wrong ones. She'd confessed to Dot that she liked living a bit farther from the epicenter of the ranch, simply because it gave her a place to live her own life, out of the spotlight.

Ward was one of the ranch foremen, though, and that by definition, put him in the spotlight. If she wanted to be at his side—and she did—she'd have to learn how to squint into that light.

She drank greedily and faced the pile of pavers she'd dumped from the back of Brutus. She had at least two more hours of work, and then she'd need to get the Quik-Crete mixed and poured.

The sky above darkened, and Dot looked up into it. She closed her eyes as a gust of wind kicked up, and she breathed that air straight into her lungs.

You love Ward.

You want to marry him.

It's the right thing for you. You'll get to make your own decisions still.

She and Ward had talked about her role in her business, From the Ground Up. She didn't want to lose all she'd worked for over the years. He didn't want her to lose anything either.

But she wasn't blind, and she wasn't stupid. She knew Sammy Glover still owned the small mechanic shop in town, but she didn't work there anymore. Oakley Glover still owned Mack's Motorsports, but once again, her role there was practically only on paper. Oakley went to town twice a week for a few hours, where she used to work six days a week, from open until close. Sometimes she took her baby with her, and Dot could see herself doing that.

"It's a long ways off anyway," she said. She and Ward weren't getting married until June, and she had no plans to get pregnant for the first full year of marriage. She wanted time to be with Ward. She wanted to figure out how to run From the Ground Up when her attention had to be divided between the business and her husband.

"What's a long ways off?"

Dot startled at the voice and spun toward it to find her fiancé walking toward her. He ate up the distance quickly and leaned down to kiss her. She grabbed onto the collar of his denim jacket and pulled him closer.

"Mm," he said, stroking his mouth against hers. Dot never felt more loved and more cherished and more feminine than she did while Ward kissed her. She couldn't wait to be his wife, and she thought Charlie had been the smartest of them all by forgoing the big ceremony and just getting the I-do said.

He finally pulled away first, as he usually did. "What's on your mind, Dot?" he asked, tucking her against his chest.

"Why would something be on my mind?"

"You're out here alone, talkin' to yourself, for one," he said, chuckling. "And you just kissed me like I've never been kissed before, for two."

She smiled at the horizon. "Maybe we should get married sooner."

"Sooner?"

"Like, I don't know. Next week."

Ward burst out laughing, and Dot could admit it sounded crazy. She laughed with him, but she wasn't letting go of him. "Ward, I don't want a bunch of kids."

"You've said as much."

"How many do you want?"

"I don't know," he said. "Whatever we have."

"Everyone here just seems so...."

"We're a family-oriented bunch," he said.

"What if I'm not?" She did pull away then and met his

eye. He searched her face, something in his sharpening and then softening.

"Dot, I'm not going to push you into anything you don't want to do," he said. "I told you I'd be fine with one child, and I meant it. We don't have to worry about what anyone else in the family is doing."

"Honestly?"

"Honestly."

"I feel pressure from them," Dot said. "I'm trying not to, but it's hard."

"Baby, you get to be you," Ward said. "I don't care what any of them think. I just want us to be good." He cradled her face. "We're good, right Dot?"

"Yes," she whispered. "We're good, Ward." She kissed him again, and he kept the movement slow and tender. "I love you."

"I love you too," he whispered. "I wish I could take the pressure from you. I don't know how other than to tell all the women to stop being who they want to be."

"They don't need to do that," Dot said, sighing. "I know this problem is mine."

"It's not a problem at all," Ward said. "Not for me."

"What if I feel like you're just telling me that?" Dot asked, closing her eyes so she wouldn't have to look at him.

"I don't do that, Dot," he said. "You're the one who told me I was arrogant, bossy, and opinionated. Do you really think I wouldn't voice my true feelings about this? With you?"

She shook her head and let herself breathe in the scent of him, the nearness of him. She opened her eyes and looked into his. "I think you're being honest with me."

"Good," he said. "Because I am. I honestly do not care how many kids we have. If you want one, we'll have one. I would like at least one."

"I can start with one," Dot said.

Ward smiled at her, and that gesture on his face dazzled her. "What's behind you wanting to move the wedding up?"

"Nerves," she said. "*Everyone* knows you. *Everyone* loves you. They give me the side-eye, like, 'who's that woman and why don't we know everything about her?'"

He chuckled and looked off into the horizon. "Give them time," he said. "They're getting to know you the same way you're getting to know them. It can take time, especially because I'm not as loud as some of the others around here."

"I do love them," she said. "Your family."

"I don't doubt that."

She sighed and looked out at the clouds rolling through the sky too. "Okay. More time."

"There's no rush here, Dot," he said. "I'm not going anywhere, and you've taken my whole heart. I'm yours, as long as you want me."

"I want you," she whispered.

"Good," he said, turning her toward him again. "Because I want you too." He kissed her again, and Dot released all of her worries, panic, and nerves as she focused on kissing the man she loved.

DOT LOOKED UP FROM HER PHONE WHEN THE BACK DOOR of the Ranch House opened.

"They're here," Ward said needlessly. "I'm off, baby." He stood and took his coffee mug to the kitchen sink. "Unless you want me to stay?"

Lois and Charlie entered the house, and Dot smiled as she got to her feet too. "No, it's fine," she said. Lois carried a binder in her arms, and Charlie had a couple of grocery bags dangling from her fingers.

"He's comin' with me," Preacher said, coming inside right behind the women. "Judge too. Let's go, brothers. I've got ice cream and hot fudge at my house. Well, Ward's house. The house where I currently live." He grinned at everyone, and Judge got off the couch.

"You don't have to tell me twice."

"Where's Mister?" Preacher scanned the space.

Ward picked up his jacket from the back of the dining room chair and started to put it on. "He left about an hour ago. I think he said he was going to go watch a movie with Libby and Mildred."

"Is that right?" Preacher asked. "Man, I miss a lot not being here." He glanced at his wife. "Of course, I love where I am too." He slung his arm around his wife's waist.

"Good save," she said dryly. "Go on, now. Ace is probably halfway through that bananas foster ice cream by now." She nudged him away with her hip. "Is it okay if I stay, Dot?"

"Absolutely," Dot said, pocketing her phone as Lois set down the binder they'd been working from. She took a seat at the dining room table and smiled up at Dot, who retook her seat. "What have we got tonight?"

"Okay," Lois said as the men started filing out. "The dress is well underway, and I expect to hear back from Jimena in a few weeks. Then we'll go do your first fitting."

"How many fittings do people normally do?"

Charlie unpacked the bag, and she put a single-serving container of sugar-free apple pie ice cream in front of Dot. She went into the kitchen to get spoons, and Lois said, "Oh, two or three. It's completely normal."

Dot picked up one of the spoons Charlie put on the table, and smiled at her. "I'm surprised you buy ice cream when you make it."

"Not in the mood to work tonight." She gave Dot a tired smile. "Preacher's been putting me to work on the ranch."

Surprise darted through Dot as she pried the lid off her ice cream container. "Does everyone have to work the ranch when they come up here?"

Charlie grinned and took a bite of her ice cream. Lois started to chuckle, and Dot put a bite of the cold treat into her mouth. "No, Dot," Lois said. "You don't have to work the ranch when you come live up here." She reached over and patted Dot's hand.

She sighed and enjoyed the sweet apple flavor in her mouth. "I'm a little worked up about a few things," she said.

Lois's eyebrows went up. "What things?"

"I just...my whole life is going to change with this wedding, isn't it?"

"Yes," Charlie said simply.

Lois glanced at Charlie and then back to Dot. "You love Ward, don't you?"

"Yes," Dot said. "That's an easy question." She waved her spoon. "How many kids I want, and what will happen with my landscaping company, and if I can handle everyone up here when I don't feel well—those are all things I can't answer."

Lois smiled kindly at her. "Dot, you don't have to know the answers to any of those things right now. All you need to cling to is your love for Ward. When I first married Stone, I was only twenty-one years old. I'd grown up in Three Rivers, out on a small, poor farm my father worked with his brother. Shiloh Ridge was massive to me. It scared me that I'd essentially swapped out my father's ranch for my husband's—which he worked with his brother."

Dot took another bite of her ice cream, fascinated by stories like this. Charlie likewise seemed keen to keep Lois talking.

"But the ranch here was bigger, and Stone and Bull had hired help. They worked from dawn until dusk, and sometimes through the night. I did the best I could to figure out how to take care of my husband, the house, and a ranch full of animals, fields, and cowboys. I had no idea what I was doing." She got a faraway look in her eye for a few seconds. "I forgot who I was for a while. I was just Stone's wife. Oh, this is Lois, Stone's wife. *Stone's wife* will feed us lunch. *Stone's wife* will know what to do for a sprained ankle."

Charlie and Dot exchanged a glance.

"I had Bear after fifteen months of marriage. Then

Cactus came along very soon after that. Then Judge. At that point, I either needed to figure out who I was and if I could really keep living this life, or something had to change."

"What changed?" Dot whispered.

"I did," Lois said simply. "I started by leaving my three boys under the age of five with their father for the entire day." She smiled. "I prayed all day long that they'd all still be alive when I returned, and you know what? They were. Stone wept and begged me never to leave him alone with the children again. I told him I would absolutely leave those three boys with him again, and any other children we had. That *I* needed to come before the ranch. That his children needed to know he loved them *more* than the ranch."

"Wow," Charlie said.

Lois leaned forward. "Now, you two ladies are married to the foremen of the ranch—or you will be very soon." She smiled at Dot. "Your men will work the way my Stone did. It's up to you to decide how you want your life to be. Yes, there are emergencies where concessions are made. But if you want to be first in Preacher's life, and you want to be the most important thing in Ward's life, then you'll come to a point where you'll have to do something drastic."

Charlie cleared her throat. "Preacher said Bear and Ranger have stepped back. Would Preacher or Ward do that?"

"I don't know what the future holds," Lois said softly. "Shiloh Ridge is about three times as big now as it was back then. The family is growing and growing, with babies and new spouses every month, it seems." She smiled fondly. "I love each and every one who comes to this family, for I know the amount of sacrifice and patience it takes—or that it will take. You ladies can always come to me, and I will try to help you the best way I know how. I won't tell anyone you don't want me to tell. Sometimes it's nice to know that someone has experienced the same things you are. That someone understands."

She glanced down at the binder. "I understand."

"Thank you, Lois," Dot said, and Charlie echoed the sentiment. "That means a lot." She did want and need someone who could help her when she felt alone and afraid.

"Okay." Lois drew in a breath. "Tonight, I thought you could decide what you'd like to serve for dinner at the wedding. And then the cake. Two simple choices." She flipped a few pages, and the possibilities she'd listed looked anything but simple.

"Chocolate," Dot said before Lois could even start outlining what she'd gathered together. "I know I want chocolate cake."

Chapter Seven

L ois Parker hummed to herself as she shelled edamame. She adored this salad with all the fresh vegetables, the crunchy Chinese noodles, and the tangy, sweet apple dressing. She thought about Dot, and the amount of sugar in the dressing.

She frowned, but her song didn't waver. She'd simply need to find some new recipes so Dot would always have something delicious to eat at these luncheons. She'd checked and double-checked with the woman to make sure she was coming to this luncheon, which had been postponed by a few days because Holly Ann had brought Gunnison back to Shiloh Ridge on their original luncheon date.

It was practically March, but Lois had refused skipping the February luncheon. She saw her children quite often, as her boys seemed to need her more now than they ever had in the past.

They brought their wives, their children, and their troubles to Lois's table, and she was grateful to have them all.

"Will you save me some of that?" Don asked as he entered the kitchen.

"Yep." Lois pressed into his touch, enjoying the light kiss he placed on her temple. "Are you going over to Bryan's?"

"Yes," he said with a sigh. "I don't know what to tell him." He reached for his thermos. "He's in this weird place where he wants to stay married, but he doesn't want to have to change to do it."

"Hm." Lois tried very hard not to comment on Don's children and their choices. He did the same for her. They loved one another, and they supported one another. When her kids came over, he was attentive and kind. He didn't give unsolicited advice. She did the same for him and his children.

"Liv moved out, didn't she?" Lois asked, finally finishing the last pod of edamame.

"Yes." Another sigh. "Bryan's beside himself, but again, he doesn't want to acknowledge that his unwillingness to go to therapy was her deciding factor in leaving."

"Can you tell him that?" Lois looked up from the salad and picked up the bag of kale.

"I've tried," Don said. "It goes in one ear and out the other."

Lois gave him a sympathetic smile. "Well, perhaps just sit with him and listen to him talk. Oh." She stepped over to the fridge. "And take these ham and cheese pockets. He can put them in the microwave or the toaster oven. They're good for breakfast, lunch, or dinner."

Don grinned as he took the bag of pastries Lois had made the day before. "He'll be so grateful. I think he's eating takeout for every meal—which he can't afford." He shook his head. "No judgment. Just listen."

Lois grinned at his positive self-talk and watched her husband leave the house. She did miss living up at the ranch, but she sure did like running to the grocery store in less than eight minutes. If she forgot something, it wasn't unfixable, and she didn't have to improvise.

She did consider herself a master improviser, but today's meal had come together quite nicely. She'd always cooked for a crowd, and the women coming to town that day were no different. No, they didn't wear big cowboy hats or shiny belt buckles. Most of them didn't even own boots. But they had big personalities, and big appetites, and strong friendships with one another that Lois wanted to continue to foster and build.

She thought of Sammy, and instant love filled her heart. Bear had always led the family, and when he stayed single, so did everyone else. Cactus, of course, had been married previously, but he'd suffered such a huge setback that Lois hadn't been sure he could ever properly heal.

Bear's ability to find Sammy and somehow convince her to marry him had healed Cactus in a way Lois had prayed for. It had helped Ranger stand up for himself. It had helped Bishop get serious about the right woman for him, not just the prettiest woman who would text him back.

Lois would forever be grateful to Sammy for how she

loved Bear. All of the women who loved her sons held a special place in Lois's heart, and she couldn't imagine life without them.

She turned from the salad and lifted the lid on the pulled pork. The savory scent of roasted meat met her nose, and she smiled. There was nothing quite as Texan as barbecued meat. She stirred the barbecue sauce on the stove and pulled a bowl of sweet pea salad from the fridge.

"Ding dong," Dawna called, and Lois spun from her work in the kitchen.

"Dawna," she said. She hustled through the living room as the other woman limped inside. "Where's Etta? Or Ida?"

"Oh, I had the center bring me," Dawna said, turning to close the door. Lois finally reached her and steadied her with her hand on her arm.

"You should've called me. I would've sent Don." She'd known Dawna for fifty-five years now. The woman was as stubborn as she was kind, and as she turned, Lois was once again reminded of their age.

She hugged Dawna fiercely for some reason, and the two of them stood there, just inside the door while so many memories flooded Lois's mind. "I've missed you," she whispered. "We've been through so much together, and I feel like it's ending."

Dawna held her tightly too. "That's because you have this new life with Don." She pulled back slightly. "How is he, by the way?" She smiled fondly at Lois. "You two seem so happy together. Makes me think I should tell old Chester than he can take me dancing if he'd like."

She giggled as much as a seventy-four-year-old woman

could, and Lois beamed at her. "I hope you don't think I'm too busy for you."

"I don't," Dawna assured her. "You've always treated me like a sister, Lois, and I appreciate that." She hobbled into the living room and sat down. "Now, I'm going to sit right here, and I expect a baby to find it's way into my arms."

"Holly Ann is coming with Oakley and Sammy," Lois said. "I'm sure she'll bring Gun. He's barely a week old, and she'll need to feed him with the added drive and all."

"Perfect," Dawna said. "I've only seen him the one time at the hospital."

"No," Lois said, passing her on the couch so she could go mix the barbecue sauce with her pulled pork. "Ace said they came by when they took the baby up to the ranch." She frowned at Dawna, who looked so confused for a moment.

"Oh, you're right. I did see them a couple of days ago."

"Mm." Lois didn't want to think Dawna's mind was going already, but it certainly could be. She did tell stories Lois had heard before, but Mister did that too, and he was only thirty-five years old.

Lois's mind wandered to Liberty Bellamore and what she knew of the situation between her and Mister. Her son had told her a little bit, and Lois had tried to listen and be sympathetic. She really wanted to knock some sense into her son with a rolling pin. Maybe then he'd see that through his friendship with Libby and asking her to set him up with so many *other* women, he'd hurt her.

She'd learned that Mister wasn't really serious about dating anyone, and she had no evidence to show that he was ready to buckle down and get serious with her. She was merely trying to protect herself, as she'd mentioned her feelings to Preacher when she hadn't meant to.

"How are things at the center?" Lois asked. "Did you go to that pottery class?"

When Dawna didn't answer, Lois turned her attention back to the living room. She'd leaned her head back and fallen asleep. Alarm pulled through Lois, and she once again left her lunch preparations to go to Dawna.

She sat on the couch beside her and simply reached over and took her hand. She didn't stir, and Lois could remember sitting with her in a very similar situation, right after her husband had passed away.

Bull had lived for nine years after his brother had died, but Lois could still feel his loss completely. Dawna had been so devastated, much the same way Lois had been when her husband had passed away. Those losses left scars that never truly healed over, and while Lois had lived for almost fifteen years without Stone now, her heart still cried out for him.

"Mom?" Zona entered the house, and Lois smiled at her.

"Hello, dear." She got up and went to hug her only daughter hello. The baby bump between them brought tears to her eyes. "How's the baby?" She put one hand on Arizona's stomach and smiled at the life she felt pulsing there.

"Good," Zona said. "Listen, I came early, because I wanted to ask you something." She glanced at her aunt Dawna.

Lois led her into the kitchen, where Arizona picked up a handful of popcorn. She loved the cheddar and caramel mix, and Lois could admit she did too. The caramel sometimes stuck in her teeth, and she didn't like that.

"Zona, you're going to be a wonderful mother," Lois said.

Tears sprung to Zona's eyes. "I'm scared," she said.

"I know you are," Lois said. "I was terrified when I brought Bear home. I thought for sure he wouldn't last through the night. Now, here we are almost fifty years later, and he texts me every single day." She smiled at Zona and ran her hand down the side of her daughter's face. "How you feel is normal. Every woman feels like this, with every baby they have."

Zona nodded. "I can call you if I need help, right?"

"Of course. I've already told Don I'm going to come stay with you for a couple of nights too, if you still want me to."

Zona nodded and pressed her eyes closed. "At least the house will be done before the baby comes."

"You'll be much happier settled back into your own place," Lois said. "I do miss living with you in the Top Cottage. How's the dishwasher up there?"

"Still on the fritz," Zona said. "At this point, we're eating cold cereal and instant noodles, so it doesn't matter much." She grinned and wiped her eyes.

Lois let her hand drop as she laughed. "You are not. I know you, and you're cooking for Duke every night, because food is his love language."

Zona's smile widened, and she shrugged. "You might be right."

"Oh, I'm right." She pointed to the pea salad. "Stir that, dear, and tell me what you're really afraid of."

Zona picked up the plastic serving spoon Lois had already gotten out and took the plastic wrap off the top of the bowl. "I'm worried about everything. I like hiking more than watching movies. I like horses more than dolls. I like sports cars more than frilly dresses. No one else has a girl at all, and I don't know. It's just one more way for me to stick out and do everything wrong."

"Ida has a baby girl," Lois said, just because she could. Arizona was right otherwise; Bear, Ranger, Cactus, Ace, and Bishop were all having boys. "Girls are a huge blessing to our family," she continued. "Because there are so few of them. We need more. I hope you have as many girls as you can."

"Shut your mouth, Mother," Zona said. "I just want the one. Boys I understand."

Lois wanted to tell her she didn't understand boys any more than girls, and she likely wouldn't even when she had her own. "Every child has their own personality, dear," she said instead. "They aren't cut from the same cloth, and you'll know what to do with each one when the time comes."

"I hope so," Zona said as she stirred the salad.

The doorbell rang, but Lois didn't move this time. Etta entered with Montana, Oakley, Holly Ann, and Sammy. Today, Oakley and Sammy had their babies, as did Holly Ann. Dawna perked right up as if she'd been awake all this time, and she took Holly Ann's brand-new baby boy from her without even having to ask.

Holly Ann came toward the kitchen, and while she looked like a new mother being awakened in the night, she also glowed with a light that only motherhood could bring. "I invited my sister, Lois," she said. "I hope that was okay. She could use some female camaraderie."

"Of course it's okay," Lois said. "Everyone is welcome here."

"Did you invite June?" Zona asked, meeting Lois's eyes.

She shook her head. "I talked to Judge, and he asked me not to. I don't understand everything happening with them, but I would like to respect what he's comfortable with."

Zona nodded. "I was thinking of asking Libby if she wanted to come too."

"Mister would murder you," Montana said as she stepped into the conversation. "I heard him tell Bishop to mind his own business just the other night. Bishop laughed it off, but Mister wasn't even close to joking."

"Well, Bishop has a way of overstepping boundaries sometimes," Lois said. "I think all my sons do."

"You can say that again," Zona quipped, and the three of them laughed. As the rest of the women arrived, Lois simply basked in their spirits, in their friendship, in their love. She served them pulled pork sandwiches and the two types of salads she'd made.

She listened to them talk about their lives, their children, their husbands. She watched Dawna, who seemed full of life now, so unlike the older version of herself that she'd been when she'd first arrived.

She laughed with them. She rocked babies so their mothers could get a break. She loved every minute of her life with these women, and she thanked the Lord that He'd brought them all into her family.

When Willa started packing up, Lois's heart started to wail. "I'll bring you some coconut bread when I make it next week," she promised, taking Charles from Willa so she could zip up the diaper bag.

"I'd love that. Thanks, Lois." She beamed at her and hugged her. "I'm home most of the time these days."

Lois's phone rang, and she checked the screen to see her husband's name there. "It's Don," she said, slipping the baby back into Willa's arms so she could answer the call.

"Hey, hon," he said. "I'm wondering if I can bring Bryan back to the house with me." His voice lowered, and Lois stepped away from the others saying good-bye to Willa so she could hear better. "He's not in a great place, and I figured you'd have leftovers."

"There's lots to eat here, yes," she said. "It's fine with me, Don."

"He just needs to sleep in his own bedroom," Don said. "It'll be one night."

Lois had a feeling it would be more than that, but she honestly didn't mind. She didn't see Don's children as much as hers, and perhaps this way, she could find a way to love and serve Bryan too.

"That's okay," Lois said. "We're just finishing up here."

"I'll let you go then."

The call ended, and Lois wished her luncheon didn't have to. She hugged everyone and stood in the doorway as the last person left—Etta with her mother Dawna. She wanted to call them all back, keep them all close, and make sure none of them ever had to endure anything hard.

But Lois knew life wasn't meant to be lived like that. Life was supposed to be hard; it was supposed to test a person to see what they were made of, find out who they'd stand with and what they'd not stand for.

She couldn't protect her children, their spouses, or her grandchildren from the test. She could only pray they'd do their best and pass it with flying colors.

Chapter Eight

Montana Glover put one hand on one rung of the ladder and called, "Bishop?"

"Comin'!" her husband called back to her. She couldn't get up and down the ladder anymore, and it drove her crazy. She hated being literally grounded, and she'd argued with Bishop for two weeks before finally agreeing to stay off the rooftops.

He appeared above her, the March sunlight haloing him as he peered down at her. "What's up, babe?"

"I have a call with the counter-fitter in ten minutes," she called up to him. "Then I'm going to call Micah Walker."

That got Bishop to come down the ladder, concern written in the set of his mouth and the glint in his eyes. "You don't think you can finish?"

Montana rolled her neck as Bishop put both hands on her shoulders. She really didn't want him touching her right now, and she backed up a step. He got the hint and dropped his hands back to his sides.

"We're not going to finish this house before the baby comes," she said, gesturing to the ladder. "I know it. You know it. Everyone knows it." She hadn't spoken to Arizona or Duke yet, but Zona came by the house every single day, and she had to know. Or at least suspect.

"If I call Micah, he'll be able to come finish this so Zona and Duke can move in before *their* baby comes." Montana sighed, the sound full of frustration. She felt like she and Bishop were always making promises they couldn't keep. Yes, they always made sure to keep the family updated as to how things were going, and they always put out the disclaimer that anything could happen with construction. They had to deal with someone else's schedule, get permits that could take a while, blah blah blah.

She loved her life at Shiloh Ridge Ranch. Montana really did. But right now, with a baby due in just two weeks, she was nothing but exhausted.

Purely, utterly, completely exhausted.

Tears came to her eyes, and she didn't try to hide them from Bishop the way she might have once upon a time. "Baby," he said, drawing her into his embrace. He stroked her hair and whispered, "Make your calls and go home, okay? You can take a nap, and I'll deal with Aurora after school and go get dinner."

"Will you?" Montana asked, her voice made of only emotion.

"Of course." He pulled away and ran his hands down

both sides of her face. "I love you, baby, and I think today should be your last day."

Montana wanted that as much as it horrified her. "Zona will never forgive me."

"Of course she will." Bishop smiled at her kindly. "I'll talk to her so you don't have to." He pressed a kiss to her forehead. "Do you really think Micah can come finish up here? If I have to do it alone, we'll be even further behind."

"He mentioned that he had some space in his schedule," Montana said, sniffling and pulling back her emotions with a deep inhale. "You haven't heard from the Lowensteins?"

"I have," Bishop said. "They can't come right now."

Montana nodded, trying to hold everything together. "I hate feeling like this."

"I know you do." Bishop reached up and lifted his cowboy hat. He wiped his hand through his hair and reseated his hat. "You won't be pregnant forever. You've worked hard this whole time. We only have a couple of weeks to go."

"If Micah can't come, I can ask him for the names of some people who can," she said. "I won't leave you high and dry, because we got that permit for the Kinder Ranch clearing, and that has to be done soon, or we'll lose our spot with the Cement Kings."

"I'm aware of the schedule." Bishop smiled at her. "The Lowensteins will be here by then. You're a queen, and I love you. Now, please, go home to make your calls. Close and lock the bedroom door. Take a bath. Sleep. Ignore us all for a while. We'll all be fine."

Montana thought of her daughter. Aurora was seventeen years old, and she'd graduate from high school in only three short months. Then she'd be gone. Off on her own in the world, with a scholarship to Oklahoma State University.

Montana felt like her life existed on two poles. On the right, she'd already raised a daughter. On the left, she was just barely starting a family. She didn't know how to make the two halves of her life match up, and that alone took a great mental toll from her.

"Okay," she agreed, and Bishop's eyebrows went up. She smiled at him and pressed her lips to his. "Don't look so surprised."

"You never agree with me out of the gate," he said, sliding his hands up her arms and back down. He put both palms on her belly and smiled down at their baby. "I adore you with my whole soul. Please go take care of yourself and let me take care of you."

She pressed her eyes closed so the tears wouldn't come out and nodded. Bishop went back up the ladder, and Montana did exactly what he'd advised her to do. She went back to the lovely house that sat against a bluff and behind the renovated barn—her house. The one Bishop had built for her with his bare hands and the love of his heart.

Because she wasn't as quick on her feet as she'd once been, she barely arrived in time for her call with Wiz, the counter-fitter she'd contracted with for Zona's house. "Howdy, Montana," he drawled. "I think you're goin' to sing my praises today, lady."

Montana smiled as she sat down at the desk in the

office she and Bishop shared for all the construction around the ranch. "Am I? Keep talkin', Wiz."

"I have two of your top five choices in stock, ready for installation in only twelve days."

"You're kidding." Montana clicked to wake the computer, and Zona's spreadsheet sat there, waiting for her. "Which two?" She clicked on the bottom of the sheet where it said COUNTERS and the options spread before her.

"I've got the gray quartz," he said. "Enough to do the whole house. Kitchen, all four bathrooms. The mud room. All of it."

"That's amazing by itself," Montana said, highlighting the cell and turning it light green.

"If you think so, you're gonna love me for what's coming next." Wiz chuckled while Montana didn't dare hope for their top choice. Zona really wanted the all-wood countertops, as she'd opted for all-white cabinets below. With the pewter pulls, she wanted the end grain butcher block countertops in the dark finish. Montana had been praying for them to be in stock for weeks, just as Zona had.

"I've got the Hardwood Lumber countertops you wanted."

"The end grain?" Montana's heartbeat bounced like a rubber ball through her chest.

"Those are the ones."

"Dark or...?"

"All finishes," he said. "We actually do that here in-store, so if she wants the dark stain, it's hers."

"That's phenomenal," Montana said. She highlighted the cell with the end grain in it and turned it green too.

"Do you want to call her? See what she wants?"

"I know what she wants," Montana said. "Write us up for the butcher block. Everywhere?"

"Kitchen and mud room," Wiz said. "We don't normally see the butcher block in bathrooms. So let's do the dark quartz in the bathrooms, and the butcher block in the kitchen and mudroom." Montana started typing as Wiz outlined the schedule, the deposit required, and repeated back her order.

"This is so great," Montana said, thinking this news would soften the blow that Zona wouldn't be able to move in as soon as she'd anticipated.

Bishop had been working on hiring another couple—the Lowensteins—but they couldn't come for a couple more weeks. Montana needed help *now*.

Once the call ended, she quickly dialed Micah Walker. If she could get someone to come replace her, perhaps all the news for Zona would be good.

A woman answered with, "Walker Designs," and Montana smiled.

"Simone," she said. "It's Montana Glover."

"Ah, Montana," she said, her smile now evident in her tone. "Micah said you might be calling."

"He did?"

Simone giggled and said, "He said the last time he saw you, he was surprised you were still climbing ladders."

"Well, I'm not anymore," Montana said. "What are you doing, answering his calls?"

"I've been too sick to work in my shop, and Trap's a nightmare out there. So I'm taking a little break."

"That's what I need to do too," Montana said. "Micah said—wait. Are you sick?"

"Micah and I are expecting again," Simone said easily. She started to laugh, and Montana grinned at the sound and the news.

"That's so great, Simone," she said.

"Yeah," she said. "It feels like a real blessing for us. For a while there, I wasn't sure I'd be able to get pregnant again."

"I'm very happy for you," Montana said. She had no idea what the future held for her and Bishop either, but she knew one thing: Simone had spoken true. Babies were a real blessing.

"Thanks," Simone said again. "And let's see...yes, Micah will be back tomorrow afternoon, and he doesn't have anything on his schedule for about a week. Ten days, maybe. Then he's got a consultation, and then he's starting a build out on a ranch a little east of here."

"Can I have him for those ten days?" Montana asked. "Bishop has all of the specs, the schedule, all of it. I just can't do the work."

"He's all yours," Simone said.

Relief like Montana had never known filled her. She sat back in the desk chair, her lungs emptying of air. "Thank you, Simone. You and Micah are a real life-saver."

"Oh, honey, you're saving me from the man smothering me to death." She laughed again. "Don't get me wrong; I want him here with me, but I don't need him constantly asking me how I'm feeling." Something crashed on her end of the line, and she said, "Oops, Trap just knocked over a lamp. Gotta go."

The call ended immediately, and Montana smiled to herself. She didn't miss the days of toddlers getting into trouble, but at the same time, she couldn't wait to experience them again.

With things falling into place so neatly, Montana only needed to make one more phone call before she could take the nap she desperately needed.

She dialed Zona as she sent up a prayer of gratitude for a good husband and good friends to step in and help when she needed them.

"THANKS," MONTANA SAID TO HER DAUGHTER AS Aurora held open the door to the homestead so she could enter. She carried two gifts, one for each little boy celebrating his birthday today. It wasn't actually Stetson's or Wilder's birthday on this very day, but Oakley and Sammy had planned a joint birthday party for the family to attend. They'd be celebrating the boys' individual birthdays in their own individual families.

Montana liked that, because while she loved living on the ranch with the huge, loud Glover family, she did want to keep some things private.

She waddled into the kitchen, Aurora following her, and found more balloons than she'd ever seen in one place. Blue, green, and yellow, they floated throughout the kitchen, they'd been tied to every chair, and a whole net of them had been secured to the ceiling above the living room.

"Oh, wow," she said, trying to take in everything at once. Etta worked in the kitchen, carefully pouring crushed up cookie crumbs into a rocked off section of the birthday cake she was working on. She brushed them up against the toy truck she'd stuck in the frosting before glancing up at Montana.

"That is the most amazing thing I've ever seen," Montana said, her awe yawning wider. "Did you seriously make that?"

"I did." Etta beamed at the cake and then back at Montana. "They're putting the gifts down at the end of the picnic table."

Montana handed the gifts to Aurora, who went to put them where they belonged. She'd sewn a cape for Stetson, as the little boy loved to pretend he was a superhero. He made the cutest noises with his mouth when "fighting off the bad guys," and since his name started with an S, the cape was practically a replica of Superman's.

He was turning two next week, but he had the spirit of a much older person. He loved everyone, and Montana loved him. Right now, he played happily in the living room with a blue balloon while Wilder, the other birthday boy, bounced in his toy seat.

Oakley entered the house from the back door and shrugged out of her jacket. "Charlie's on her way with the ice cream," she said. "And Willa says she's two minutes out with the other cake."

"Is that one for Wilder or Stetson?" Montana asked, taking a seat at the bar.

"This one is for Wilder," Etta said. "He loves trucks. I think Willa made a Big Bird cake for Stetson."

"No," Sammy said, entering the kitchen with her baby on her hip. Russell was starting to round out and look more like a baby instead of a newborn, and Aurora returned and took him from Sammy as she continued. "It's the Count."

"Ha ha ha!" Stetson said, followed by what should've been "I am the Count." But he wasn't even two yet, and with the accent he tried to do, it sounded more like "I-muv-Coun. Ah-ha-ha!"

Everyone started to laugh, Montana included.

All of the cowboys would arrive soon for the party, and Montana was looking forward to eating lunch and then cake and ice cream. It hadn't been as hard as she'd anticipated to let Bishop and Aurora pamper her, and she'd enjoyed her first week off.

"How are you feeling, dear?" Lois asked, and Montana hadn't even seen her arrive. She took the barstool next to Montana, her smile infectious and kind.

"I'm hanging in there," Montana said, glancing toward the arched entryway as Willa entered carrying a massive cake. "She needs help."

Several women dashed over to help her, and Montana ended up rising to her feet so they could slide the cake onto the counter without having to go around her.

Count von Count smiled out at them, and Sammy stepped next to Montana and put her arm around her. "It's perfect," she said, her voice filled with tears. "He's going to love it so much." She turned to Willa. "Thank you, Willa. I'm just helpless with things like this."

"You can fix any car," Willa said. "You could do this." She smiled as she hugged Sammy back, then turned to take her baby from Cactus, who'd entered with the boy in his arms.

"All right," Cactus said, clapping his hands together. "Let's get this party started."

Chapter Nine

Charlie Glover still had a hard time signing the right name on the dotted line. Contracts, checks, receipts. No matter what, she couldn't believe she'd become a Glover so quickly.

She was beyond grateful that she had, because staying with Preacher over the holidays and having to go downstairs to a lonely, drafty bedroom had been no fun. Sleeping in his bedroom, with him nearby, was a lot better.

She stirred her tea and kept reading the Internet article one of her gamer friends had sent her. She'd been mentioned once already for her role in the chemistry consultation, which was why Harbinger had texted her the article.

Her alarm went off, and Charlie drained the last of her morning tea. She'd already done her broadcast for the day, and she didn't have plans for an evening gaming session until next week.

Etta had hosted the March luncheon yesterday, which meant the fridge at the Ranch House where Charlie lived had plenty of food in it. She liked that, because she wasn't great in the kitchen. Or at least, she didn't like spending much time in the kitchen.

She liked making ice cream and watching the chemistry that happened while she cooked, but thinking about what to make for dinner exhausted her. Thankfully, Preacher wasn't a finicky man, and she could make grilled cheese sandwiches and open a carton of the organic roasted red pepper and tomato soup she bought at Wilde & Organic and he'd be happy.

He left ultra-early for work out on the ranch, but he came home quite early in the day too. Usually about three o'clock, he'd come into the Ranch House, strip off his boots and jacket just inside the door, and find her in the living room waiting for him.

He'd shower, and they'd spend the rest of the day together. It was a good life, and one that Charlie wanted to embrace for as long as possible.

She silenced the alarm and put her teacup in the sink. Nothing in the Ranch House felt like hers, and she reminded herself that she had a long way to go before she'd be living in a house that actually was hers.

For now, she and Preach lived in Ward's house. Once Arizona and Duke's house was complete on the Rhinehart Ranch, they'd move there, leaving the Top Cottage empty.

Charlie and Preacher would then move there until their brand-new homestead on the old Kinder Ranch land was complete. They were getting new barns, new cowboy cabins, new roads, and new equipment sheds.

Preacher and his crew of cowboys and cowgirls would live down there, and Charlie would finally have a place to call home. It didn't bother her that much to be moving around for right now.

She still had her house in the hills, though she had contacted a real estate agent last week. It was a huge house, in a rich, gated neighborhood, and Marcus had told her they might have to be patient to find just the right buyer.

Charlie was in no hurry, because she had enough money to pay the mortgage on the house.

Paulie meowed and jumped up onto the counter, clearly looking for a crumb Charlie might have left behind. "Get down," she said to the cat. "I'm going to help Montana and Bishop this morning, and y'all better be good."

She glared at Archie, her second cat, as he came prowling into the room. "There's a cat door right there." She indicated the addition to the Ranch House she'd installed on the sliding glass door. "Go catch a mouse or two."

Her cats weren't really outdoor cats, a fact that hadn't escaped her attention once she'd moved them up to the ranch with her. The first time she'd put Archie on the front lawn still made her smile and then laugh.

The feline had frozen. Literally, frozen, as if he'd never felt the blades of grass against his delicate paw pads before. Archie was so fussy, but at least he stayed off the counter.

With April almost upon them, the weather had warmed

to the point that Charlie could go outside without a jacket. She'd been helping Montana with Zona's house for a couple of days now, doing whatever the other woman asked her to.

Micah Walker had come to help, and he'd kept them on schedule. Montana was on strict orders from her husband to only *oversee* things, and she only worked a few hours each day.

Charlie liked spending time with Montana, because while she was petite, with blonde hair and blue eyes, the woman was really a powerhouse. She knew every detail of building a house, and that fascinated Charlie, whose mind simply didn't work that way.

She made the drive up the road toward the Top Cottage, and then past the fence line that separated Shiloh Ridge from the Rhinehart Ranch. The service road between the two properties could use some improvements, but Charlie always drove her truck when she went this way.

The house came into view the moment she turned left, and the road improved as she went further onto the Rhinehart Ranch. A few trucks were already parked in front of the house, but Arizona's wasn't one of them.

A couple of men worked up on the roof, and Charlie shaded her eyes as she looked up there. Montana wouldn't be up there. She didn't lift a hammer anymore. She simply came to the worksite to oversee things, and she'd joked with Charlie that she was going to do all of her projects that way from now on.

Charlie entered the house through the front door, immediately pausing as she took in the sheets on the floor. "Looks like the painters are getting ready," she called.

"Yep." Montana's voice came from a room just off the entrance. She'd set up a six-foot table in there, and she looked up as Charlie entered. "Heya, Charlie."

"Heya, Montana." Charlie went to the only other chair and sat down. "Where do you want me today?"

Montana slid a clipboard across the table. "I've got the rest of the cabinets going in today. I need you to get the delivery guys to sign those. And the main guy—Tommy? He has to sign the front one saying the work is satisfactory and complete before he leaves. I'll inspect them before he does."

"Okay," Charlie said, glad she didn't have to inspect anything. She wouldn't even know what to look for.

"We should be getting the panel put on the outdoor electrical box," Montana said. "Did you see an electrical truck out there?"

"Nope." Charlie knew enough to know what a utilities truck looked like. She flipped a couple of pages. "Oh, the extra driveway pad is being poured."

"Yes," Montana said. "It should've been done with the driveway, but Zona and Duke added it later. They should be here this afternoon. I'll be gone by then, so I'll need you to run point with them. They're easy." She went on to detail that Charlie just had to get a signature, make sure they poured in the right spot, and then let them do their work.

She did a lot of observing and standing around, honestly. But it if helped Montana, Charlie was willing to do it. "What about lunch?" she asked. "I can run to town and pick something up."

"Wade said he'd bring in lunch today," Montana said with a smile. "Whoever's here can eat it." She leaned forward, a grimace crossing her face. "I hope I'm here, because Sally's a great cook."

"Is that his wife?"

Montana nodded. "She makes the best chicken hand pies in the state."

"My mouth is watering already," Charlie said.

"That's because you're still drinking SlimDown for breakfast," Montana said. "I don't know how you do it."

"It's good," Charlie said. "I don't like to cook, and Slim-Down sponsors my show."

"They do?" Montana's eyebrows went up. "I didn't know that."

Charlie shifted in her seat, but she told herself she wanted to share these kinds of details with the ranch wives. "Yeah," she said. "It didn't start out that way, but I drank one on every morning broadcast, and when I got big enough, they offered me a sponsorship."

She'd have to tell the women on the ranch details like this if she expected to be close with them. And she did want to be close with them. She saw the bond between Sammy and Oakley, and she knew Montana spent a lot of time with Holly Ann. Preacher sort of revolved around his own sun, and that meant Charlie did too.

But she'd really like to deviate from the course and find someone she belonged with too. Willa had always been kind to her, and she'd spent a lot of time talking to Dot at the few luncheons she'd attended.

When it was her turn to host the luncheon—not until

September, thankfully—she'd have to share something about herself no one knew, and she figured she'd start practicing now.

"That's great," Montana said, and it sounded like she meant it. "Did you ever talk to your sister?"

"Yeah," Charlie said. Davie had called yesterday while Charlie had been helping Montana make sure the fireplace got bricked exactly right, and she'd run out to take the call. "She just wanted to tell me that she's met 'the most dreamy man,' and she needed to tell me all about him."

Montana giggled with her, and then she said, "I remember the magic of meeting an amazing man. It is fun."

"It is," Charlie agreed. "She wants me to go down to Dallas to meet him. I told her she has to know him for longer than a week before I make that trip." She laughed again, though she did love her twin sister. Sometimes, it felt like they weren't cut from the same DNA at all. Other times, Charlie knew exactly what was going on in Davie's head before her sister even called.

The grumbling of an engine reached her ears, and then loud beeping, indicating a truck was backing up. She stood and turned to leave the makeshift office. "I'll go see who that is."

"Might be my cabinets," Montana said.

Charlie opened the front door and sure enough, an enormous delivery truck with a rocking chair painted on the side came to a stop. "It's the cabinets," she called to Montana.

A man got out of the cab and waved to her. Charlie

went down the front steps, leaving behind the wide, beautiful porch that faced south. Duke and Zona would have plenty of sunshine in the winter months, that was for sure. "You must be Tommy."

"Nah," he said, reaching her and shaking her hand. "He's right behind us though. We're puttin' these in the kitchen?"

"Yep," Charlie said. "Right through the garage there."

Another man started to open the back of the truck, and Charlie assumed her role of standing there watching them work. Another truck—a regular pickup—arrived and this time, Tommy did get out of it. Four other men did too, and they got to work actually installing the cabinetry.

The delivery guy signed the delivery paperwork, and the behemoth of a truck left. Charlie went inside, because while the house didn't have heat or air conditioning turned on yet, it was cooler inside than standing out in the sun.

She'd just taken in the shell of the kitchen, envisioning where all the cabinets would go and how the space would look once they were in, when Montana yelled, "Charlie? Are you in here?"

Something alerted inside Charlie's mind. "Yes," she called, turning away from the cabinets and jogging through the living area to the hallway that ran toward the front door.

Montana appeared there, one hand heavy against the doorjamb and one pressed to the top of her pregnant belly. "I just had a contraction," she said, her face turning white right in front of Charlie.

Charlie dropped the clipboard as she raced the last few

steps to Montana. She went to her knees, panting, and Charlie knelt in front of her.

"There's something wrong," Montana said, groaning immediately afterward. "It wasn't like this the first time."

"What do I do?" Charlie asked, panicking. She'd never been pregnant. She didn't know what to do. "Call Bishop? An ambulance?"

"Get my phone," Montana said, lifting her eyes to Charlie's. She was so strong, and so brave, and Charlie wanted to be just like her.

She drew in a breath and blew it out. "Let's start toward the hospital. We don't have time to wait for an ambulance." Charlie got to her feet and strode toward the table, where Montana's phone sat. "Got the phone. Let's go."

She couldn't get Montana to her feet alone, and she whistled through her teeth and called, "Tommy!"

He appeared a moment later, and the three of them got Montana out of the house, down the steps, and into the passenger seat of Charlie's truck. She ran around to the driver's side and got behind the wheel.

With her heart pounding, she said, "I'm calling Bishop."

"Another one is starting," Montana said, her voice tight. "The first one came in at ten-fifty-two. What time is it now?"

"Ten-fifty-eight," Charlie said.

"Six minutes," Montana said, her eyes pressed closed and both hands holding her belly now. "We've got time."

"Do we?" Charlie asked, punching at the phone to get it to dial Bishop.

"Yes," Montana said, her voice whooshing out as she exhaled. "They're not very long, and they're still quite far apart."

"Should we be going to the hospital then?"

"Yes," Montana said firmly. "There's something wrong."

Charlie reached the end of the dirt road and turned onto the highway, Montana's phone finally connecting the call to Bishop. She glanced at Montana as the line rang. "How do you know?"

"I don't think the baby has dropped or turned," she said quietly. "I didn't think I was ready to have the baby, but I couldn't pinpoint why. Now I know why." She spoke in a haunted voice, and while Charlie wasn't entirely sure what she meant by the baby not being in the right position, she knew the feeling of fear and dread seeping into every cell in her body.

"Hey, baby," Bishop answered.

"It's Charlie," Charlie said. "Montana is having contractions about six minutes apart."

Montana's hand came down on her arm, and Charlie looked at her friend. "Don't tell him about the baby. Just tell him to come."

Charlie nodded, not sure what Bishop had just said. "She wants you to come meet her at the hospital. We're on our way there right now."

"I'm on my way," he said, and the call ended.

Charlie handed the phone back to Montana and gripped the wheel with both hands. "Okay, Montana. I'm right here, and you're going to tell me when you have another contraction." She looked at the clock, then her rear view mirror. "We'll time them, and we'll get you to the hospital, and everything will be okay."

Her voice broke on the last word, and she reached over and took Montana's hand in hers. Her fingers gripped back as hard as Charlie's did, and she said, "Do you want to say a prayer?"

"Will you?" Montana whispered. "Then I need to call my daughter too."

Chapter Ten

Aurora Martin swept away her mom's phone call, because she was in the middle of a chemistry test. Confusion made her frown, and not only because of the complex problem on the paper in front of her.

Why was her mother calling her in the middle of the morning? She knew Aurora couldn't answer and talk. Her mom had Aurora's school schedule memorized, and she knew she didn't have lunch until twelve-thirty-seven.

She glanced at her phone again, noting that it was just after eleven o'clock in the morning. *Odd*, she thought.

She looked around the classroom, but all the other students were bent over their tests, tapping on their phones or calculators to do the math, and coloring in bubbles.

Her phone started to vibrate again, and this time, Aurora stood up and collected her phone, her test, and her pencil. She swiped on the call and whispered, "Just a sec, Mom," as she walked down the aisle toward her teacher.

"What's goin on, Miss Martin?" Mrs. Pittard asked. She frowned deeply, but the woman seemed to be able to do that by barely moving her face.

"It's my mom," Aurora said. "She's called twice, and she's pregnant, and she'd never interrupt me like this if it wasn't important." She turned over her test. "I have to go talk to her."

Mrs. Pittard hesitated, looking like she didn't know what to say. Aurora wasn't going to wait for permission. She hitched her backpack higher onto her shoulder and put her phone at her ear. "What's wrong, Mom?"

"It's Charlie, Aurora," Charlie said. "And you're right. Your mother is going into labor, and she'd like you at the hospital."

Aurora told herself not to break into a run. "Okay," she said. "I'm on my way right now."

"She says she'll call and excuse you when she can."

"It's fine."

"I'm not going to tell her that," Charlie said, clearly moving the phone away from her mouth.

"Aurora," someone called behind her, and she turned back toward the chemistry room. Oliver Osburn strode in her direction. "What's going on?"

"My mom's having the baby," she said. "You shouldn't have left. You'll fail the test."

"I was almost done," he said, and that was probably true. Oliver excelled at chemistry, because his brain understood numbers and letters in the same equation where Aurora's didn't. "Do you want me to come with you?"

"No, you stay here," she said. The last thing she needed was to get him in trouble with his parents—again. "If you come, your mom will freak out," she added in a whisper, remembering she was on the phone with Charlie. "I'll stay in touch, and you can come after school if I'm still at the hospital."

He nodded, though he frowned too, clearly not liking her solution. Aurora liked Ollie more than any other boy she'd ever known. Their relationship hadn't been perfect, and Aurora was only seventeen years old. She listened when her mom said she didn't know what love was, but she sure felt like she loved Oliver Osburn.

She'd still applied to several colleges, and she'd accepted at Oklahoma State, while Ollie had gotten into UT-Austin, where his grandparents had both gone, as well as his father and his uncle. In just a few months, they'd live in different states.

They'd talked about the various ways to stay in touch, to long-distance date, but the truth was, Aurora couldn't predict what might happen. Oakley and Sammy said she might meet someone at college who made her heart race the way it did whenever she looked at Ollie.

Willa said it was okay to keep her options open. Her mother had encouraged her to get her own skills and pursue her own dreams. If Aurora were to really do that, she'd be moving to Savannah, not Oklahoma City, and she'd be attending the SCAD for fashion, fashion marketing and management, or furniture design.

She loved being behind a sewing machine, taking something ordinary and making it extraordinary. She adored working with unique, out-of-the-box fabrics, and she enjoyed taking the things she saw inside her mind and making them into reality.

She'd told Oliver all of this, and he'd looked up the Savannah College of Art and Design. He'd found several programs he was interested in, including animation, equestrian studies, advertising, and graphic design.

They'd started talking about applying for a January start and moving to Savannah together, but nothing had actually been done. She couldn't even *imagine* what Bishop and her mother would say if she did such a thing.

In truth, Aurora couldn't even imagine herself doing what she and Ollie had fantasized about. She wasn't a huge risk-taker, and she didn't want to cause any problems for her mother, who'd always been there for Aurora.

Tears pricked her eyes. "Stay here, please," she whispered to Ollie. "I'll be in touch, I promise." She tipped up onto her toes and kissed him right there in the hallway.

He kissed her back, and Aurora didn't care how young they were. Kissing him sure felt like falling in love with him.

HALF AN HOUR LATER, AURORA STOOD AS BISHOP entered the maternity wing. "Bishop."

"Baby," he said, and Aurora rushed at him. He wasn't her biological father, but he loved her the way a dad should love their daughter. Her own father was completely absent in her life, and she'd been so grateful for Bishop over the past few years.

"Charlie came out a minute ago," she said as Bishop took her into his arms and held her tight. "She said you should go back the moment you arrive." She stepped back and wiped her eyes. "She said Mom might have to have a C-section. The baby isn't in the right place."

"Okay," Bishop said, stepping back a single step. He took her face in his hands. "It's going to be okay. I'll go back right now. Are you okay here?"

Aurora nodded and sniffled. "Charlie said she'd come out when you got here and sit with me."

"Okay, baby." Bishop spoke in his easy tone, but he wore his nerves in his expression. He pressed a kiss to her forehead and said, "I called Uncle Bear, so the whole family will be here soon enough."

She smiled at him and nodded. When he stepped past her, she turned to watch him, folding her arms across her stomach. "Bless my mom," she prayed right out loud. "Bless the baby coming that he'll be okay."

She grabbed her phone when it started to ring, and she swiped on Aunt Jackie's call. "Hey," she said. "Bishop just got here."

"Praise the Lord," Aunt Jackie said. "We're on the way, girlie. Everything will be okay now, ya'hear?"

"Yes, ma'am," Aurora said, though she felt like one wrong breath would crack her chest wide open. "I'm going to tell Ollie to come after school."

"That's fine, honey," Aunt Jackie said. "Uncle Bob is getting you a cinnamon roll."

A smile spread across Aurora's face. "Thanks, Aunt Jackie."

"I love you, honey. Be there soon."

"Yep." Aurora tucked her phone into her back pocket and walked toward the door Bishop had gone through. She peered through the tiny window and turned away again. "She's going to be fine. The baby will be fine."

She considered herself a very positive person, but worry gnawed at her guts. Oliver could help her feel better. Aurora got out her phone and forced herself to take a seat. *You could come after school if you don't have to work. My mom is probably going to have to have a C-section, so I'll be here all afternoon.*

I'll call my uncle at lunch, Ollie said almost instantly. *Need me to bring you anything?*

My aunt is bringing me a cinnamon roll, so I think I'm good.

I'll get you the Summer Lovin and bring it with me.

Aurora smiled at the mention of her favorite soda pop. It came with raspberry syrup and cream, and she did love it.

Did she love Oliver Osburn?

On some level, she really thought she did. She didn't know how to bring it up with her mom or Bishop, and as Aunt Jackie bustled into the waiting room, Aurora wondered if she could talk to her aunt about her feelings for the tall, handsome boy who would be a man soon.

"Any word?" Aunt Jackie asked, taking Aurora into a hug and looking toward the nurses' station.

"Nothing yet," she said.

"I'm going to go check." Aunt Jackie hurried away, and Uncle Bob extended the cinnamon roll toward Aurora with a smile.

"How you hanging in there, bud?" he asked.

"Good." She sighed as she took the treat and sat back down. Uncle Bob sat beside her, and when Aunt Jackie returned a few minutes later, she said, "She's having a C-section. They're getting her ready now. They expect to have the baby delivered in only twenty minutes or so."

She sat and put her purse on her lap, her eyes wide and filled with concern.

"Twenty minutes," Aurora said. "That's not too long."

Turned out, it could take twenty years for twenty minutes to pass when one was waiting for something so nerve-wracking and exciting.

Thirty minutes passed. Then forty.

Aunt Jackie stood, but Aurora put her hand on her aunt's arm. "He'll come out when he can."

As if bidden by her statement, Bishop came through the doors, and he carried the baby in his arms.

Aurora exploded to her feet and ran toward him. "How's Mom? How is she?"

"She's so great," Bishop said with a smile. He put his arm around Aurora. "She had a C-section, baby. She's gonna need a lot of help when she comes home."

Tears flowed down Aurora's face. "I can help her, Bish."

"I know you can, baby. Meet your brother." He passed the baby to her, and Aurora gazed into the infant's perfect face. "We named him Robert." Bishop looked up as Aunt

Jackie and Uncle Bob arrived. "You two mean so much to her."

He stepped over to them and hugged them simultaneously. Aurora couldn't look away from the tiny human in her arms, noting his lack of chin—just like hers—and his very prominent Glover nose.

"Hello, Robbie," she whispered, leaning down to kiss him.

"Incoming," Bishop said. "Bear brought the crew."

Aurora turned to see Bear and Sammy walking toward them, along with Oakley, Ranger, Ward, Etta, Zona, and Ace. "Don't worry, Aunt Jackie," she said. "I'll make sure you get him next."

Chapter Eleven

❦

Driving up the lane to Shiloh Ridge Ranch used to make Liberty Bellamore smile. Now, it brought a quiver to her stomach she didn't know how to soothe. Mister Glover had been down to her house a couple of times since the Valentine's Day dance where she'd stood in the safety and comfort of his arms and fantasized about what it would be like to be his.

Libby existed within the realm of reality, and she wasn't convinced that Mister really wanted to settle down with anyone. He was simply jealous of his brothers and cousins.

"And he's lonely," she told herself, something Mildred had suggested he might be.

Of course he was lonely. Libby knew that. She could feel it in his texts and see it on his face when she saw him in person. She knew what loneliness felt like, and it was watching her best friend go out with woman after woman, most of whom he'd asked her to set him up with.

It was giving him a piece of her heart with every smile he tossed her way, every time he texted her, and every time he asked her out. At the rate they were going, she'd be heartless by summertime.

She'd fed him fried chicken and polenta last time he'd come to her house, and Mildred hadn't left her side for longer than fifteen seconds. That had frustrated Mister, but Libby didn't trust herself to be alone with him. He was so charming, and so gorgeous, and she'd liked him for so long.

If only he were serious about anything, she thought as she went under the arched sign announcing her arrival at Shiloh Ridge Ranch. She turned left, away from the homestead, and continued down the graveled roads toward the big, blue barn where the Glovers held their family celebrations. She'd attended a few of their parties and a couple of their weddings, and she knew her way around this ranch.

She'd spent plenty of time here as a child, always running after Mister as he left her behind when they went horseback riding or when his father told him to go round up the goats and bring them into the barn.

She'd grown up working her ranch too, and Libby loved nothing more than she loved Texas, the morning sunrise, and a good day's work in a garden, field, or stable. Her two older brothers were married with children, and they were practically running the ranch now.

Libby and Mildred headed up the commercial side of the ranch, and that included the Country Christmas festival they hosted each year. A couple of Christmases ago, she'd made the grave mistake of asking Preacher about

Mister, and that had set this whole messy ball of yarn into a tangle.

She turned to go past the barn to Bishop and Montana's house, where she'd deliver her casserole, wish the new mother well, and get on home. "That's all you're here to do," she said as she eased her old, rusty pickup truck to a stop.

This truck had been her grandmother's, and Libby spent more time tinkering with the fuel pump than she'd like. Otherwise, she loved the vehicle, and whenever she went anywhere, she put the windows down manually and let the fresh air fill her life with oxygen.

She peered through the windshield at the house, noting the other cars parked out front. She didn't see Mister's truck, and his was hard to miss. Everything about the man was a cut above other men—even his brothers. His jeans were always cleaner. His boot shinier. His belt buckle bigger. His laugh louder.

His truck was huge—a King cab—with an extra-long bed. Leather seats. Matte black paint. The best of the best, that was all Mister Glover wanted.

And that meant he'd never be happy with her.

Libby wasn't a cut above anything or anyone. She'd been invisible to Mister for many years, and she didn't want his attention on her because he'd learned she had a crush on him. That wasn't how true love was built, and she wasn't going to let him play games with her heart.

She collected her chicken cordon Bleu casserole and got out of the truck. She reached back inside for the bagged salad and box of ice cream sandwiches—all meals should include dessert, and she hadn't had time to make her raisin-filled cookies—and faced the house again.

Her stride remained strong all the way to the door, and she pressed the doorbell decisively. Voices started behind it, and Libby fell back a step.

Montana Glover herself opened the door, and a smile containing the wattage of the sun burst onto her face. "Libby, come in."

"I just brought dinner, ma'am," Libby said, though Montana could only be a few years older than her.

"Oh, don't you dare ma'am me," Montana said, stepping back. "Come put it on the kitchen counter."

Libby stepped into the house and found herself in the middle of a playdate. Awkwardness filled her as she met Holly Ann's eyes. She held her baby over her shoulder as she patted his back. Sammy had both of her boys there, the oldest playing with Oakley's son in a playpen in the corner.

Willa Glover stood in the kitchen, her baby in one arm and a bottle of formula in her other hand. "Libby," she said. "How good to see you." She smiled too, as if she genuinely enjoyed seeing Libby.

"I brought chicken cordon Bleu casserole," she said. "Sammy said Montana and Bishop love it."

"I sure do," Montana said. She took the ice cream sandwiches out of the box. "Thank you so much for these. I'm not sharing them with anyone." She laughed as she put the ice cream in the freezer. "Come sit down for a minute."

"Oh, I can't," Libby said, but Montana looped her arm through Libby's and tugged her into the living room.

Ida sat on the couch, both of her twins on the floor at

her feet. Etta, her sister, sat on the floor with them, putting a pacifier back into the little girl's mouth. "Howdy, Libby," Ida said, glancing at her sister.

"Howdy," she said, taking a seat in the straight-backed dining room chair someone had placed next to the couch. "Do you guys get together every day like this?"

"Heavens, no," Holly Ann said. "Montana came home yesterday, and we thought we'd all get together for an hour today. That's all."

"We have a luncheon once a month," Ida said, standing up. She handed Libby a bowl of foil-wrapped candy. "You should come."

Libby took the bowl and glanced up at Ida, surprise lifting her eyebrows. "I should?"

"Sure," Ida said. "It's low-key. We eat and talk."

Libby looked around the living room. Even Charlie was there, though she had no baby to bring with her. "With all of you?"

"My mother comes too," Ida said. "Aunt Lois does. Zona's usually there."

"Where is she today?" Libby asked, selecting an orange-wrapped chocolate. She was fairly sure it was a caramel one, and she did adore caramel and chocolate together.

"She's moving a few things into her house," Montana said with a sigh. She sat on the end of the couch as Ida retook her spot in the middle. "It's not done yet, but she wants to get everything over that she can before her baby comes."

"She's due when?" Libby asked, peeling back the wrapper on her chocolate.

"End of April," Sammy said. "Another month or so."

"Then the babies will be done for a while," Willa said. She'd taken the recliner, and she gently moved herself back and forth as she fed her baby.

Libby could admit that being here with these women soothed the ragged edges of her soul. They were all kind, and they were all welcoming, and they were all married to a Glover or had been a Glover themselves at one point.

Libby was neither of those things.

"Yep, done with babies for a while," Oakley said. "Ward's getting married, though, so there's that to look forward to."

"Unless Charlie has something to say," Sammy said, smiling at the other blonde.

"Nope," Charlie said, flashing a tight smile back to Sammy. She didn't say a whole lot, and Libby found herself smiling at the woman.

"Where's Dot?" Libby asked.

"She works a lot," Charlie said. "She comes to the luncheons if she can."

Libby nodded, because she wasn't sure what she was supposed to say next. She'd always been fairly good at small talk and making others comfortable, but this situation felt seven shades of wrong to her.

"I need to get going," she said. "I told my sister I wouldn't be gone long, because we still have planting to do." She stood and handed the bowl of chocolate back to Ida.

She wore a panicked look as she took it, and she said, "Etta."

"You invited her," Etta said. "What would you like me to do?"

Montana rose too, a groan coming from her mouth. "You really could come, Libby," she said as she followed Libby to the front door.

Libby turned back to her, feeling fierce and strong. "Why would I, Montana? It's clear it's a luncheon for Glovers, and I am not a Glover."

Anxiety bloomed on Montana's face, and the wail of a baby saved her from answering. Libby didn't need to hear the answer anyway. It was humiliating enough knowing that they all knew about her and Mister's relationship troubles.

While Montana turned back to the group of babies, mothers, and sisters-in-law, Libby opened the door and slipped out of the house.

THE NEXT DAY, LIBBY HAD JUST POURED HER RANCH dressing over her salad when someone knocked on the cabin door. Mildred looked up from her lunch too. "I know who that knock belongs to."

"He hasn't texted." Libby stood, confused as to why Mister would come to her house without talking to her first. He never did that.

"Libby," he called through the wood. "Are you there? It's Mister."

As if she didn't know. Libby called, "Coming," and took the last few steps to the door. She opened it, surprised to see Mister standing there even though she knew it would be him. "What are you doing here?"

He wore the widest smile to go with his wide shoulders in that blue and black plaid shirt. He was everything Texas cowboy that Libby had always wanted, and she wished her crush on him would evaporate. She'd asked God to take it from her, just pluck it clean from her soul and let her live in peace, but He hadn't.

She had to live with these intense feelings of attraction day in and day out, and Mister sure didn't make things any easier for her by showing up looking so dang good. He smelled good, and he laughed like he was the happiest man on earth because he was with her.

"What's going on?" she asked, unable to contain her own smile. "You're grinning like a fool."

"Remember that article I submitted to *Modern Rodeo*?"

"Yes," she said. She'd edited it for him, during one of the times when they were getting along.

"It got accepted today. I got the email while Judge and I were driving back to the ranch, and I made him detour here so I could tell you." He laughed as he reached for her. He lifted her right up off the ground and spun with her. "Thank you for helping me with it."

She giggled too, the feel of his strong hands on her waist and back like a touch straight from heaven. "Of course."

He set her back down and glanced toward the kitchen. "Howdy, Mildred."

"Hello, Mister."

"Can I steal her for a second?"

"You already have," Mildred said in a deadpan.

"Great." Mister didn't mind Mildred's salty attitude, and he laced his fingers through Libby's and tugged her out onto the porch.

"Steal me where?" she asked. "I need to eat lunch and get back out in the tractor. Christian wants to plant tonight, and that means I have to get the fields plowed under."

"I won't keep you for long," he said, taking two or three steps to the left. "We're just going right here."

A big, brown truck waited down the road a bit, the back of it facing the house. "Is Judge waiting for you?"

"Yes," he said. "That's why this won't take very long."

As much as Libby liked the solid, warm feel of his fingers between hers, she gently tugged her hand away from his. "What's 'this,' Mister?"

He paced away from her and turned back, his dark blue eyes wide and filled with trepidation. She knew what was coming. Another of Mister's speeches. She really didn't have the time or patience for them anymore, and instant irritation sparked within her.

"When I got the email, Libs, you're the first person I wanted to tell. Heck, you're the *only* person I wanted to tell. I came straight here, because I wanted you to know. We worked so hard on that article, and I wanted to share it with you."

She pressed her back into the logs of the cabin as he returned to her. He put one hand on the wall near her head. "Please," he said. "I'm serious about us. I think about you day and night. Everything that happens, good or bad, I want to share with you. When some stupid chicken lays a pink egg, I think, 'Libby would like this.' I take a picture of it to send to you, for crying out loud. Then I second-guess it and don't send it."

He took a deep breath and brushed a loose lock of hair from her face. She pulled in a tight breath as fireworks popped through her cheek where he'd touched. Why was she fighting her feelings so hard? Why was she fighting Mister so much?

"You're everywhere for me, and I don't know how to prove to you that I'm serious. I'm not just looking for a good time, though I think we'd have an amazing time together."

Libby drew in a breath filled with the scent of his ranch, his cologne, his skin. "What do you want from me, Mister?"

"I want a chance," he whispered, dipping his head closer and closer to her. "Just a single chance, Libby."

"I've already given you a couple of chances," she said.

"I didn't know about them."

That was exactly why she didn't want to open her chest and let him remove her heart with his bare hands. How could he not know?

Her knees trembled and her eyes closed as his hand slid down the side of her face. He curled his fingers around the back of her neck. "I'd like to kiss you right now," he said. "But last time I tried, you slapped me. Can I?"

Libby was so tired of fighting. So tired of resisting. What would happen if she just gave in to him? To herself?

She didn't know, and she wouldn't find out unless she

took a leap of faith. So she said, "Yes," and drew in a breath only a moment before Mister's lips touched hers.

This kiss was far different than the one he'd tried to take from her at the New Year's Eve party. That had been rough, demanding.

This kiss was gentle and tender. This kiss sought permission to go deeper, and Libby found herself giving it. This kiss held adoration and love, and Libby hadn't been kissed like this, by anyone, in a very long time. If ever.

She wanted to kiss him for a lot longer, but Mister pulled away. He breathed in through his nose and said, "Thank you, Libby," before touching his cheek to hers. "Would you go to dinner with me tonight?"

Seeing as she'd already given him her heart with a single kiss, she had nothing left to lose by saying, "Yes. Dinner sounds great."

Chapter Twelve

"Enough with the pictures," Arizona Rhinehart said. Honestly, how many photos of her pregnancy did she need? Not this many.

"Okay," Dot said, lowering Zona's phone. "I'm sure we got a good one for your eight-month album."

Annoyance flashed through her, though it wasn't Dot's fault. Zona had wanted a month-by-month journey through her pregnancy with photos. She'd had someone different take them for her every month, and as she'd gotten to know and love Dot in the past few months, it felt perfect to have her take the second-to-last set.

For her nine-month picture, Zona was going to have Duke be on the other side of the camera. He'd been right beside her through everything, even when she wasn't very nice to him when he offered to bring her her shoes and tie them for her.

She hated feeling helpless, and being eight months

pregnant had limited her in ways she'd never anticipated—including tying her own blasted shoes.

She couldn't wear her cowgirl boots anymore either, and that sent another flash of irritation through her.

"Thank you," she said as kindly as she could. She took her phone from Dot and faced the boxes she'd been working steadily to pack.

Every morning, Duke rolled over when his alarm went off and kissed her. He'd murmur how much he loved her, and then he'd shower and go make coffee. She usually fell back to sleep while the water ran in the bathroom, and woke sometime later to a cup of coffee on the nightstand. Weak coffee, as the stronger stuff made her stomach ache and the baby go a little crazy.

Duke put in plenty of cream and sugar, though Zona had never taken it that way on her own. Her taste buds had changed a little bit in the past year or so, and during her pregnancy, she couldn't get enough salt no matter what. Nothing had any flavor, in her opinion.

"One box at a time," Dot said. "Where are you putting these at the new house?"

Everyone knew the house wasn't done yet. That frustrated Zona too, but she certainly couldn't fault Montana or Bishop. They'd been working on it non-stop for months. Montana had been limited by her own pregnancy and the birth of her son, and though she'd brought in Micah Walker for a couple of weeks, the house still wasn't finished.

"In the garage," she said. "That way, once we do move in, I can just go through them a little at a time."

Dot toed one of the boxes. "You don't need any of this stuff?"

"It's mostly clothes, books, and stuff like camping gear and Christmas decorations."

Dot looked at Zona. "You decorate your own house for the holidays? More than what y'all do at the homestead?"

"I do," Zona said. "Mother loved it, and so did I, so when we lived together here in the Top Cottage, we always put up a few things." She smiled at the good memories. She missed living with her mother, though being married to Duke was a new kind of bliss all its own. There was nothing as magical as waking up next to the man she loved.

"Will I have to do that?"

Zona expanded her smile. "Dotty." She put her arm around her, though Dot hated the nickname that only Zona called her.

"I'm not sure I'm cut out to be one of you."

"Come on," Zona said, in complete disbelief. She looked at Dot just to make sure she wasn't kidding. She didn't seem to be. "The first thing you need to accept is that you get to do whatever you want. If you don't feel like coming to Sunday dinner? Don't come. A few people might ask, but not because they're judging you for not coming, but because they care about you and miss you."

"Like you didn't go over to Montana's after she brought Robbie home."

Dot hadn't gone either, and Zona nodded. "Just like that. You don't have to be them, Dot. You don't have to be me. You don't have to do anything you don't want to.

When invitations are put out, that's all they are: invitations. There's no obligations in the Glover family."

Dot nodded, but she still wore a dubious expression. Zona couldn't explain it any better than she had, and Dot would figure things out for herself once she truly joined the family and had the new last name.

Zona squatted to pick up one of the boxes she'd labeled light. "I'm only taking the ones that don't weigh much," she said. "I marked them."

"Smart." Dot got to work too, and with the help of Brutus—who could hold so much more than Zona's truck —they only had to make one trip from the Top Cottage to the new house that sat right on the edge of the Rhinehart Ranch.

Duke's parents had given them an acre to build their house for their family, as Duke would be taking over the ranch once his father finally decided to retire.

He'd left Three Rivers for a while after some dark years, where he said and did things he'd been ashamed of for a very long time. Sometimes, he still had flashes of regret, and Zona tried to remind him that everyone had regrets and things in their past they wished they could change.

Once Dot put down the last box, she groaned and stretched her back. "Next time you ask for help, I'm going to get details first."

Zona laughed, and it felt good to wash away some of her negativity, especially when Dot joined in.

"What's your plan now?" Dot asked, turning away from the three-car garage which would only fit two cars with the number of boxes Zona had brought over from the Top Cottage.

"Lunch?" Zona asked. "I could hitch a ride with you and Brutus to town and Oakley could bring me back when she leaves Mack's." She pulled out her phone to call Oakley, her eyebrows raised.

"You never have to ask me to lunch twice," Dot said.

"You have time?"

"I took today off," Dot said. "Ward's meeting me at the floral shop with Lois at two o'clock."

Zona looked at her phone. "Plenty of time for lunch then. What are you thinking about for the flowers?"

ARIZONA ROLLED OVER IN BED, THOUGH IT WASN'T nearly as easy as it had once been. She actually had to do it in three shifts, like a triangle.

"You okay, hon?" Duke asked, his voice low in the darkness. It was probably close to time for him to get up to go to work on the ranch.

"I just can't get comfortable," she said, keeping her voice low too. "I'm just going to get up."

Swinging her legs over the side of the bed used to be easy too, but now she had to use her hands to brace herself up.

Pain ran through her back, shoulders, and midsection, and she froze. She pulled in a breath while Duke also sat up on his side of the bed.

She'd never been in labor before, but she was the last

ranch wife to have her baby, and she'd listened to Montana's and Holly Ann's stories.

"I'm going to get in the shower," Duke said, yawning.

"Okay," Zona said, though she wanted to call him back and tell him she might be going into labor.

"No," she whispered. Her baby girl wasn't due for another three weeks. She wasn't coming today. She couldn't.

The house wasn't done. Arizona and Duke hadn't moved yet. They weren't ready for their baby to come.

Zona got to her feet slowly, which she'd had to do for several mornings in a row now. Nothing new there.

The throbbing in her lower back was new, though. Holly Ann had had pain in her lower back.

Zona checked, and her water hadn't broken. The bed was dry, as were her pajamas. She made her way into the kitchen and got down the bottle of acetaminophen. She'd be fine once she had a little juice and took some pills.

The baby wasn't coming today. She couldn't.

By mid-afternoon, Zona couldn't get off the couch due to the radiating pain in her back. It moved around her like a plane circling the globe, rippling across her stomach and making her press her palm to the muscles there that were so very unhappy.

She'd been crying for ten minutes, begging God to stop what she knew deep in her heart were labor pains.

"I'm not ready," she said, weeping. "We don't have a

name picked out, and I don't know how to do hair, and I'm not ready to be a mother to a girl."

She thought she had more time.

"We haven't moved yet," she said. "Please."

Someone knocked on the door, and Zona could only turn her head in that direction. She couldn't get up to get the door, and she knew with sudden clarity that she needed to call Duke and face facts.

"I'm coming in," Charlie said. "Are you here, Arizona? Your truck is out front." The blonde woman appeared in the doorway, took one look at Zona, and rushed toward her. "Hey, hey, are you okay?"

She knelt at the couch in front of Zona. "Where's Duke? I've driven one woman in labor to the hospital. I can do it again."

Zona cried even harder, hating this weak feeling inside her. She'd been caging it for years, and she hated the loss of control.

"I'm calling Duke," Charlie said.

"Baby," Duke called, and he walked into the house in the next moment too.

"She's in labor," Charlie said, rising to her feet. "I was outlining my next demo, and I just had this feeling that I should come check on her."

"Duke," Zona said, the name more of a whimper.

"It's okay, baby," he said, coming to her side. "Let's get you into the truck." He looked at Charlie. "How long has she been like this?"

"I don't know," Charlie said. "I just got here. I was going to call you when you walked in." She wore fear on her face, as did Duke, and Arizona wondered what they saw when they looked at her.

"All day," Zona managed to say as Duke helped her up. The pain burst through her then, and she realized she'd not been feeling it fully as she'd been coiled into herself.

"Maybe during the night," she said. "I've had pain in my back since I got up this morning."

"Why didn't you tell me?"

Zona met her husband's eyes, pure panic filling her. "I'm scared. I'm not ready."

"We're ready," Duke said.

"What if I—" Zona couldn't finish her question, but the truth was, she was terrified she wouldn't love her baby girl. She hadn't wanted a girl, and she couldn't really say she wanted one now. They'd done three ultrasounds just to make sure the baby was indeed a girl, and every time, she was still a girl.

"Come on, hon," Duke said kindly. "It's time to go to the hospital." He took control then, and Zona didn't mind relinquishing her tight grip on things to Duke.

The drive to the hospital seemed to take no time at all, and Duke checked on her every time she groaned. As he shouldered her weight while they walked in, he said to the first receptionist he saw, "She's in labor. Contractions every three minutes."

From there, Zona did whatever anyone told her to do. She let Duke help her into a gown. She let the nurses hook up monitors. She told the doctor she was ready to deliver the baby, though she wasn't.

She sort of disappeared inside herself and let everyone

else do what they needed to do. "Arizona," Duke said, his face appearing only a few inches in front of hers. "Snap out of it. It's time to push."

She blinked once, then twice, and then nodded. "Okay."

The lights, sights, sounds, and noise in the delivery room rushed at her, and she met the doctor's eyes. "Now?"

"On the next contraction," Dr. Myers said, glancing at the monitor. "Here it comes." He didn't need to tell her, because Zona could feel the tightening and pressure.

"Now," he said, and Zona pushed. After only four contractions, the doctor said, "And here she is."

The tiniest cry filled the air, and Zona's chest collapsed in on itself. That was her baby. Her daughter.

Her heart filled with love, and she sobbed. The doctor held the baby up and then handed her to a nurse.

"One more push, Zona," he said, and she did that while the nurses attended to her daughter. Panic started to fill her again that she didn't have her baby yet.

"Where is she?" she asked, though she could still hear the infant fussing.

"Here you go, Daddy," a nurse said, and she handed a pink-swaddled bundle to Duke.

"Oh." Arizona couldn't look away from her husband and that baby, and her entire being filled with joy. Love and joy.

It overflowed and overflowed, and when Duke tilted his arms so she could get her first look at her daughter, Zona knew without a doubt that she loved her with every particle of her body and mind that new how to love.

She reached for her, and Duke passed their baby to her, then pressed his lips to her forehead. "You did great, hon. I love you so much."

She gazed down at her daughter, and she suddenly hoped that every baby she and Duke were blessed with would be a girl. "What are we going to name her?" she whispered. "We never decided."

The baby whined and then wailed, and Zona laughed. Duke did too, adding, "I think she's going to have your spunk, Zona. What about naming her after your grandmother? Priscilla?"

"I do like that," she said. "But I don't want to call her that."

"Of course you don't," Duke said dryly. "You want Shiloh."

"What about Priscilla Shiloh?" she suggested. "You get the traditional family name you want. I get the more modern name that still means a lot." She looked at him, hope in her heart that he'd agree.

He smiled at her, and he was so beautiful. She distinctly remembered meeting him for the first time after he'd returned to Three Rivers. She'd known of him growing up, but he was eight years older than her, and they certainly hadn't been friends or attended any of the same schools at the same time.

He was just as beautiful now as he was then. More, even.

"Welcome to the family, Priscilla Shiloh Rhinehart," he whispered, leaning down to give their precious daughter a kiss.

Chapter Thirteen

Ida Burton now knew how to budget her time. She knew it took twenty minutes to get out of the house with both babies. She knew how to get them into the double sling in under five minutes. She knew to take the large diaper bag if she was going up to the ranch, and the small one if she was just running to the grocery store.

Since the twins had been born, along with the house where she and Brady were raising their kids, Ida only went to the ranch or the grocery store. She hadn't been shopping in months, and the weather had kept her from walking the trails in the parks around town.

Today, though, Ida was going to take the twins to the mall. Alone. For the first time.

Etta had been coming to help Ida a couple of days a week, and she hadn't even gone to the grocery store without her sister. They'd gone to visit Mother in the care facility too, so Ida supposed she did go other places besides the ranch or to get more milk.

"All right, Judy," she said to her little girl. "You're in first, because Johnny hogs all the room." She smiled at her son, who smiled back at her and then promptly toppled over.

She giggled at him but let him fuss as he rolled onto his back. The babies were three months old now, and Johnny definitely did outpace Judy in development. He'd been sitting up for a day or two, though he obviously wasn't very good at it. He weighed a pound more than his sister, and he'd already started vocalizing his first sounds.

Judy smiled at Ida, and she was definitely a thriving, beautiful baby. She couldn't sit up on her own yet, and she was definitely much quieter than her brother.

"We're going shopping today," Ida said, strapping Judy into her car seat. "Dot is marrying Ward soon, and we're having a bridal shower for her this weekend."

She took Judy out to the car and locked the car seat into the base. She opened the garage and started the car to get the air blowing. Texas was in this weird stage where it wasn't warm enough for air conditioning, nor was it cold enough to run the furnace. She still wasn't going to leave her baby in the car without some sort of air blowing. Her car allowed her to set a temperature and it would blow hot or cold air to keep the car that temperature. She turned that knob to seventy degrees, and said, "I'm going to go get Johnny. You hang tight here."

Judy, of course, didn't respond. Ida went back inside to find Johnny yelling for her. Sort of.

"Da, da, da!" the little boy babbled.

"Daddy's at work," Ida told him. Brady did work a lot, and Ida had thought she'd been prepared for him to continue his role in the police department.

She'd been wrong. She was slowly learning how to do things by herself, support her husband, and allow him to be the father he wanted to be when he was home.

She wasn't very good at it, and she and Brady had endured several discussions together. Things changed all the time, but she knew two things: Brady loved her, and she loved him. And secondly, Brady loved his children and wanted to be their father.

She'd thought about telling him he didn't need to work so much, but a big part of who Brady Burton was came wrapped up in his job as a lead detective on the police force in Three Rivers.

She'd told him before that they didn't need the money. She and Etta worked the ranch the same as her brothers and cousins. They'd gotten an equal cut of the inheritance, even if they didn't don hats and go move sprinkler pipes. They brought students and the community to Shiloh Ridge, and they educated many about what ranches did and how vital they were to the American way of life.

With Johnny in the car, Ida got behind the wheel and took a moment to take stock of everything she had.

The small diaper bag. Her twin sling. The double stroller. Her wallet. Her phone.

"All right," she said. "We're ready."

She made the drive to the mall with nursery rhymes

playing over the radio. She sang along with them and talked to the babies as if they could talk back.

She set up the double stroller in the parking lot and put the babies in their seats. She set a timer for an hour, because she'd need to drive through somewhere for lunch and get the babies home to feed them and put them down for afternoon naps after that long.

Dot had claimed she was a simple woman who'd lived on her own for decades. She didn't need anything to get married, because Ward was a grown man who had everything they needed too.

None of the Glovers were going to let this wedding go by without a shower, that was for sure. Especially Ida. She and Ward were close, and she was thrilled he'd found someone he loved the way he loved Dot. By extension, Ida loved Dot to her very core, and that required her to find the perfect gift for her.

What that was, Ida wasn't sure. She pushed the babies past the clothing stores and the chocolate factory, though she'd like to stop there and get some caramel-filled pretzels.

She saw people looking at her, many of them smiling when they realized she had twins. Every time she took them anywhere, she got stopped, and Ida honestly didn't mind that too much.

She bypassed the jewelry stores, as that felt more like something Ward should buy for Dot.

Since Dot was diabetic, Ida didn't want to give her a food gift. She entered the home good store, because Dot had commented that she liked the wingback chair that also reclined in Ida's living room.

Ward didn't have anything like that in the Ranch House, and one of Ida's happy places was a store that had chairs, pillows, and lamps.

Dot loved dogs, and Ward had been educating her about horses, cows, and the ranch. When Ida's eye caught a throw pillow with a black lab on it, she detoured that way, taking a path that went the long route around due to the big stroller.

"We need this pillow," she told the twins. "I mean, Dot needs this pillow." She browsed through the chairs, got someone to help her, and finally found the perfect chair to go with the perfect black lab pillow. It would fit in the living room at the ranch house, but if Dot didn't want it in there, she could put it in the office she and Ward were planning to share.

"I'll take these three things," Ida said, nodding to the chair, then the two pillows she'd selected. She couldn't help herself with the second pillow. It was a long, lumbar pillow that had the definition of *blessed* on it.

Since Ida felt blessed beyond measure, she wanted the reminder of it in her house. If she didn't have a couch or chair to put it on, she'd simply put it on the front table.

"Do you have cash?" the clerk asked. "Our Internet is down." She looked apologetic. "We've got someone here fixing it, and she says it'll only be a few minutes. I can hold these things for you while you look around." She glanced at the babies. "Or whatever."

Ida took out her phone and looked at it. "I have a few minutes," she said. "I can wait."

"Great," the clerk said. "I'll take these up front for you." She took the pillows, and Ida looked at a couple of sets of dishes before following her.

"June," she said, instantly recognizing the woman behind the long check-out counter. "You're fixing the Internet."

Juniper Nichols looked up, her frustrated expression changing to recognition and then melting into a smile. "Ida, heya." She wiped her bangs back out of her face.

"You cut your hair," Ida said, taking in the shorter hairdo. "I really like it."

"Thanks," June said. "I'm not sure I'm in love with it yet, but it's what I've got." She reached for a tool on the counter. "I'm almost done, I swear."

"You're fine," Ida said, latching onto the idea that she'd run into June for a reason. She'd been working hard to listen to her feelings and the promptings she believed came from the Lord.

Last week, she'd invited Libby Bellamore to the ranch wives' luncheon, but she hadn't agreed to come. Montana had said that Libby knew what the luncheons were, and she didn't belong.

Ida still wished she'd come, because she had a strong feeling Mister and Libby would end up together. Maybe not soon. Maybe not right away. But they definitely belonged together, and if it was anywhere in God's plan, Libby would be a Glover one day. She might as well come to the luncheons.

"Listen, June, are you still seeing Judge?"

June's head whipped up, her eyes wide.

"Oh, I see," Ida said, wishing the Lord would give her more tact. "Listen, I don't—"

"I want to see him," June said, leaning forward. "I'm just...really bad at dating. Really bad at letting someone in."

Ida blinked, because she hadn't anticipated June giving her any details at all. *Help me know what to say.*

She opened her mouth, her faith full and strong. "Maybe you'd like to come to these luncheons we have with all the ranch wives. I'm sure we could help you with a solution for how to deal with Judge. We all know him fairly well."

June searched her face. "Really?"

"Sure," Ida said, smiling. "We get together once a month, anyone who can. No obligation, of course. Someone hosts at their house, and when they do, they provide the meal." She swallowed, because she wanted June to come so badly, and she wasn't even sure why.

"The host usually tells us one thing we don't know about them," she said. "That way, we get to know each other. We support each other. The cowboy way of life up at that ranch is hard, and it's important that we all know we're not alone."

"That sounds nice," June said quietly. "Sometimes I feel so alone, and with my daughter graduating and leaving...." She let her voice trail off, and Ida could feel her loneliness pulsing through the air.

"So you'll come to the luncheons," Ida said. "We'd all love to have you. My husband doesn't work a ranch, but he works a lot, and I have these babies. I've never done much without my sister, and now I've got seven or eight other women to call on if I need help. It's really great."

June nodded and ducked back down under the counter. "If you let me know when it is, I can look at my schedule."

"Perfect," Ida said, smiling. "Do you want to ask Judge about it before I add you to our group text?"

"Try it now," June said, standing and looking at the clerk. She started clicking on her computer, and June turned back to Ida. "Yeah, I probably better run it by Judge. I wouldn't want him to think I'm going behind his back or anything."

Ida wasn't sure why Judge would feel like that, but something niggled at her mind about Preacher and Charlie. They'd texted her and invited her to the luncheons when she and Preacher were broken up, and Preacher hadn't been super happy about that.

"It's working," the clerk said, grinning at June.

June grinned too and started packing up her supplies and tools. "Great. Sorry about that. Your lines hadn't been upgraded in years."

"That's not your fault," the clerk said just as Johnny started to fuss. "Let's get you on your way, and then I'll call my boss." As she rang up Ida's few things, Ida got June's phone number and gave her hers.

"I won't add you until you text me and say it's okay," Ida said. "I know you'll be welcome at the lunches, but I don't want you to do anything that makes you uncomfortable or that jeopardizes your relationship with Judge."

"Okay," June said simply.

Ida paid while pushing and pulling the stroller back and forth to try to soothe Johnny. That didn't really work, but at least she got out of the home goods store and back to her car before he really started screaming.

Chapter Fourteen

J uniper Nichols really wanted to go lunch with Ida and Etta. She really did. They'd been sweet enough to invite her, and she honestly liked both twins. There had been no mention of a ranch-wide luncheon, and June actually hoped she wouldn't get invited anyway.

Yes, she'd told Ida she'd like to be included, but she'd said so in a moment of weakness. The Internet cables at All For Home, the store where she'd run into Ida a couple of weeks ago, hadn't been upgraded in a decade. She hadn't installed their system, and yet the owner there, a one Leslie Becker, had wanted June to fix everything for free.

And fast.

She hadn't spoken to Judge in a couple of weeks at that time, after he'd had to cancel because his family had called an important meeting that all Glovers had to attend. He probably thought she was upset with him, when she wasn't.

She was simply upset with the situation. She'd let life

pull her in and push her out, because business kept her running most days. She rarely had time to sit down and think, and even when she did, Lucy Mae would come in with some story about something another stupid senior had done over at the high school.

June had made a personal vow thirteen years ago that nothing—not a job, not her ex-husband, not a new man— would come between her and her daughter. She'd not dated anyone very seriously...until Judge Glover.

She'd met the cowboy almost five years ago now, and the fact that he was still interested in her spoke volumes. It could fill archives.

And she was equally as interested in him.

June looked down at her phone again. *I can't go to lunch on Friday*, she typed out for Etta and Ida. *I have to work that day.*

Saturday then, Ida said. *Brady has the whole weekend off. I'll be twin-free.*

Etta chimed in with, *I can't Saturday. I have lunch plans already.*

Lunch plans? Ida asked. *With who?*

The conversation morphed right before June's eyes, and an uncomfortable feeling that she was reading someone's private discussion pulled through her. Thankfully, Etta didn't answer, and the thread went dormant. At least one of them had realized she was still able to see their texts.

She wanted lunch plans on Saturday too, and June swiped and tapped before she could think too hard about what she'd just done.

"Juniper," Judge Glover said in lieu of hello. "To what do I owe this great honor of getting your call?"

She smiled just hearing his voice. It was deep and rich and so full of Texas, she expected him to beam the star right from his chest. She settled more fully into the front seat of her work van, where she still sat after pulling into the driveway at least ten minutes ago.

Lucy Mae's car wasn't there, which meant she was either at work or out with her boyfriend. June searched her memory and came up with work. Her daughter worked at the automatic car wash in town, and she always had a great story to tell when she came home.

"June?" Judge asked. "Did I lose you?" The phone scratched, and he said, "I think I lost her."

"I'm here," she blurted out.

"Oh, can you hear me?"

"Yes," she said.

"Did you mean to dial me?"

They hadn't spoken in so long, he thought she'd accidentally called him. A pocket dial. She cleared her throat. "Yes," she said. "I meant to call."

"What can I do for you?" He always asked what he could do for her, and it was a little nod to how she answered the phone at Nichols Networking. She had a list a mile long for what Judge could do for her, but the most pressing issue sat right at the tip of her tongue.

"I was...this is going to be so weird."

"What is?"

"I'm not on speaker, am I?"

"No," he said. "I'm just finishing dinner with Ward and Mister. I'll go downstairs."

June frowned, though she wasn't sure why. Something about him going downstairs.... "Why do you have to go downstairs?"

"That's where my bedroom is. This feels like a call you want to have in private."

"I am sitting in my work van," June admitted. "Though Lucy Mae isn't home. I know the moment I walk in, Picasso and Remmy will demand to be fed."

"Those dogs are ferocious," he teased.

June laughed lightly, and it actually felt amazing. The heavy weight she'd been carrying lightened. "Listen, one of your cousins asked me if I'd like to come, I don't even know, hang out? Hang out with them up on the ranch. Sometimes. Or something. They do luncheons, I guess?"

Why couldn't she even say a sentence around this man? They weren't even in the same room together.

"Ida," he said as if he knew.

"It was Ida," she said.

"Do you want to go hang out with them?"

"I would if you were okay with it."

A long pause came through the line, and June pressed her eyes closed and said a quick prayer. *Please don't let this be why we can't be together.* Had she just blown things with him by asking to spend time with his female cousins and sisters-in-law?

"Why wouldn't I be okay with it?" Judge finally asked.

"Well, you paused for about an hour," she said. "So there must've been something you were thinking about."

"There is," he said slowly. "I just...you know what? I'm just going to say it."

"Okay."

"We've had a hard time getting together, right?"

"Right."

"I get that it's neither of our faults. Life is crazy sometimes. But here you are, calling me essentially to ask if you can come up to the ranch and spend time with *the women*." He cleared his throat, and all the dots connected for June.

"I'm so sorry," she whispered. "Of course, when I have time to come to the ranch, I want to see you."

"Do you, Juniper?" he asked, that sexy, sultry voice so low, and yet so cutting at the same time. "You can do whatever you'd like, sweetheart. I'm not going to tell you yes or no to whether you can attend the monthly luncheons with Ida and the other ranch wives."

Ranch wives.

June pulled in a shaky breath. "What's your schedule like this weekend?"

Judge let out the breath she'd pulled in, and she did the same, imagining for a moment that they were in the room together. He'd take her into his arms and dance with her, and June would forget about the no-good week she'd had at work. She wouldn't worry about sending Lucy Mae halfway across the country with her father. She would only have pine-scented things in her life, and strong arms, and that voice telling her that she best not say things she didn't mean.

"We're driving our herd out into the range starting tomorrow," he said. "I'll be off the ranch until Tuesday."

"Oh."

"I'm sorry," he said. Something hung in the air, and June waited. "There's a big dinner on Tuesday up here at the ranch." He spoke slowly, deliberately. "It's a welcome-back party for those of us who go out on the range. There's lots of food and a big bonfire. You could come, if you'd like."

Instead of just blurting out the word, "Yes," June cocked her head and tried for flirty. "Depends," she said. "Do you shower before the party? Or is this literally you sliding from the saddle after being gone for four days without bathing?"

Judge burst out laughing, and June could've closed her eyes, died, and gone to heaven the happiest woman in the world from that sound alone.

"Tell you what, June-Bug," he said. "If you commit to coming, I'll shower first."

"I'll be there," she said.

"Great," Judge said. "And June, I mean it. If you want to do things with Ida and the others, do them."

"I'll just tell them they can add me to their texts," she said. "They seem to do most of their activities in the middle of a weekday."

"Ah, yes," he said. "I'm sure they do."

June had a job. A very busy business to run. She couldn't just stop everything and go to lunch because she wanted to. Heck, today, she'd eaten her leftover spaghetti pie in this very seat where she now sat, a few bites at red lights as she drove to her next appointment.

"I miss you, Judge," she whispered, almost like she was afraid to say it out loud in case it hurt more.

"I miss you too, June," he whispered back.

"Let's promise that we won't let so long go between conversations," she said.

"I promise."

She smiled as her stomach growled. "Okay." She drew another deep breath, and this time it didn't vibrate through her chest. "Tuesday. What time?"

"I think we eat at six," he said. "It'll be out at our new fire pit. If you text me when you get here, I'll come meet you at the homestead."

"Okay," she said.

"Or I can come pick you up."

"That's silly." June didn't need to make his day longer. "I'll come to you."

"All right," he drawled. "The big bonfire is after dinner. There will be s'mores and marshmallows and all of that."

"I can't wait," June said.

Neither of them seemed to want to end the call very badly, but finally Judge said, "I have to go, June-Bug. I'll talk to you later, all right?"

"All right." She drew out the words the way he did, which made them both chuckle. She hung up first, because the call was starting to turn awkward, and she didn't need that in her life.

"What I need, Lord," she said, tipping her head back and looking at the ceiling in the van. "Is Judge Glover in my life. Can You please help me with him? Please? Don't let anything come up on Tuesday night."

She just knew that if she had to cancel again, he'd write her off for good.

The Lord did answer prayers, because Tuesday was a ho-hum, normal-as-can-be day for June. She worked in her office in the morning, and she went out on one single call in the afternoon. She even had time to shower before she began the thirty-minute drive into the Southern hills outside of Three Rivers.

The road up to Shiloh Ridge had been fixed, and she went right under the arch that proclaimed she'd arrived on the ranch. She wondered if they'd move it once they finished working on the area closer to the highway.

As she'd passed, she'd noticed that a lot of work had been done since she'd been here last. The land was cleared, and it looked like new roads were going in. Foundations of cement had been poured, and they hadn't been small.

Judge had told her once upon a time that his father and uncle had bought the bordering ranch, but they hadn't done anything with it. Now, the family would be using it— after they improved the land, added a house, some barns, and a few cowboy cabins.

He spoke of things like that easily, as if anyone could redo an entire ranch without batting a single eyelash.

June had some money; she wasn't hurting, at least. But she wasn't wealthy, not the way the Glovers were. One only had to arrive on their ranch to see the money oozing from the land, and June had been here plenty of times.

She'd installed the WiFi networks in every house on this ranch, of which there were currently seven. And the barn, which of course needed WiFi for their weddings, celebrations, parties, and anniversaries.

June turned toward the barn before remembering Judge had said this particular party would be at their new fire pit. She pulled off the road and texted him, *I'm here.*

Yeah, I saw you turn the wrong way. I'm coming.

June looked in her rear view mirror and started to back up. Trucks took up every available spot in the gravel lot in front of the homestead, and she ended up parking off the side of the road just past the lane that led onto it.

She got out of the car as Judge crossed the road, a wide smile on his face. "Howdy, June."

She straightened, the wind cooling the May air enough to make it breathable. "Howdy, Judge."

"Wow, you look amazing." He took her arms in his hands and held her a couple of feet away from him as he looked down to her shoes and back to her scalp. "Amazing."

She wanted to lean into him and kiss him hello. She'd kissed him before, but it had been so very long ago. Her lips twitched, and she managed to tame them into a smile. "Thank you, cowboy. You look nice too."

He removed his hands from her body. "I showered and everything." He grinned at her and cocked his arm for her to take. "It's not far to the fire pit. You can probably hear the music."

She could, but she still let him lead the way past the equipment sheds to a beautiful oasis bordering the barn and a grassy field. A well stood among all the new pavers and gravel, as did an enormous picnic table. Two of them.

Food covered half of one of the tables, and a mother swatted away a little boy's hand as he tried to take a cube of watermelon before she wanted him to. Dogs barked in the background. A horse whinnied.

The fire started to crackle, and men and women talked.

June counted no less than eight babies, plus a couple of older boys. The two of them had their heads bent together, their hands moving through the air quickly. No doubt they were trying to devise a way to get to that watermelon without getting caught.

June's throat could use some cool, sweet watermelon about now too. She swallowed simply looking at the enormity of the group gathered in front of her. She recognized all of them, because the Glovers weren't hermits. Ace and Holly Ann did a lot of volunteer work for the Christmas Festival.

Sammy owned the best mechanic shop in Three Rivers, while Oakley owned and operated the biggest car dealership in the county. Etta and Ida ran school and community outreach programs, and Willa was the pastor at the church where June dragged Lucy Mae every week.

"Oh, Pastor Corning is here too," she said, finding the man with his two daughters after someone shifted and moved out of the way.

"He's Willa's brother," Judge said. "And Willa's married to Cactus, you remember?"

"Yes," she said, reaching for his hand. "You won't leave me alone with them, will you?"

He chuckled and gripped her fingers tightly. "Not if you don't want me to."

"I don't want you to."

"Should we jump into the fray?"

"Judge," an older woman said, and June turned to her left to find his mother had joined them. She must've come up from behind, because June hadn't seen her approach. "They're loud already, aren't they?"

"At least we're outside for this party," Judge said. He tugged June forward a little bit, not shy about holding her hand in front of all these people. "Mother, you remember Juniper Nichols, don't you?" He smiled at June. "June, my mother, Lois, and her husband Don."

"So nice to see you again, ma'am," June said.

Lois's eyebrows went up, and she looked from June to Judge. "You too, June. I've been meaning to call you."

"You have?"

"Mother," Judge warned. Their eyes met again, and they had an entire conversation without saying a word.

"June!" someone called, and she looked away from Judge and his mother to find Ida striding toward her. "It is you. Hello." She hugged June, which sent spirals of surprise sliding through her.

"Oh, hi."

"Come with me," Ida said. "I *have* to show you what the chickens and turkeys scratched up today. You're not going to like it." She didn't give June a choice, and the next thing she knew, she'd been separated from Judge.

Chapter Fifteen

Dawna Glover loved a bonfire. It warmed her body and her soul. She loved her family, even if they were loud.

Bull had wanted a big family; Stone too. They'd only had each other growing up, and the two of them couldn't work a ranch the size of Shiloh Ridge without paying for a lot of help. Instead of doing that, they'd had a lot of kids. A lot of loud, strapping boys that had become even louder, stronger men.

Nine of them, in fact, and the ranch that Dawna's husband had dedicated his life to was bigger and better than ever.

"Oh, you'd love to be here," she said to her beloved Bull.

"Can you take Gun?" Ace asked, sliding onto the bench next to her. Her sons had always been good to her, and Ace was a jewel among gems. "Holly Ann wants to dance, and I can't pass that up." His eyes twinkled like stars, and he passed his baby to Dawna.

She could sit and hold babies all day, every day, so she didn't mind. Ward had driven to town to pick her up, and he'd helped her out here to this spot where she sat. He'd put on the stadium seat so she'd have a back to rest against, and he'd faced her toward the party and not away from it.

Gun babbled in her arms, and Dawna bent her head to kiss her grandson. "Oh, you would've charmed your grampa in two seconds flat," she said, smiling at the baby. He'd been named after Bull, and that made Dawna smile every time she thought about it.

She had four grandbabies now, and she hoped to live long enough to have twice that many, and then three times that.

She watched Brady as he stood near the playpen where Ida had put their twins. She'd disappeared somewhere, the way Ida always did. Ward had gone to help Bear and Ranger start the fire, as Ward was always right there for the oldest boys who ran the ranch.

Cactus had joined that trio too, and he'd been such a good friend to all three of her boys. She loved Stone and Lois's children as if they were her own, and she knew Lois held the same love and compassion for her children.

She drew in a deep breath of the ranch air. "Oh, I miss this ranch, Bull. I'm sure you do too." She'd fallen and broken her hip a while back, and life was much easier at the assisted living facility. Leaving Shiloh Ridge had been the second-hardest thing she'd ever done. Burying her beloved Bull had been the hardest.

He was buried right here on the ranch, but she hadn't gone to visit his grave in a while. She'd ask Ranger to take her next time she came to the ranch. As if he knew she'd been thinking about him, her oldest child turned toward her.

Ranger made his way over to her, smiling at Preacher and Charlie as he went past. "Mother," he said as he sat down. "Do you want me to bring you dessert first?"

She reached over and put one of her weathered hands on his leg. "Is that a real question?"

He chuckled and shook his head. "We're going to announce the baby tonight," he said in a low voice. "Thank you for keeping it to yourself."

She had a moment where she wasn't sure what he was talking about. "Of course," she said anyway. The pathways in her mind weren't as straight as they'd once been, that was for sure.

Ranger stood up and pressed a kiss to her forehead. "I'll bring you a s'more with double marshmallow."

She grinned, because she did like that. Ranger had made it all the way back to the fire pit before she realized he'd said they were going to announce the baby. "Of course," she said, bouncing Gun on her lap. "Ranger and Oakley are expecting again."

They'd told her that; she'd just forgotten.

Her eyes caught on Etta, the only one of her children who didn't have a significant other. No boyfriend, even.

Dawna's countenance changed in a moment, as her

heart swelled with sadness and love for Etta. She didn't look lonely, but Dawna knew so well that some emotions were easy to hide. She often experienced loneliness, but Lois came to see her almost every day now that she wasn't living here at the ranch, and her children were good to her.

She tried to focus on the good things in life, not the things that troubled her. A wave of exhaustion filled her, and baby Gun in her hands started to slip. She pulled him back onto her lap as she watched Etta.

She stood with Willa and Montana, the two of them with babies in slings on the front of their bodies. Etta seemed perfectly at ease with them, but Dawna knew the way every cry and every giggle cut into her daughter.

"Please help her," she prayed right out loud. "Bull, you've always been so protective of the girls. Etta needs your help."

She could almost hear Bull asking her, *What would you like me to do, love?*

"I don't know," she murmured. What she did know was she couldn't hold this wiggly baby for much longer without dumping him on his head in the gravel.

"Howdy, Aunt Dawna," Sammy said, taking the spot next to her on the bench. "Can I take him?"

"Please," Dawna said. "Where are your two?"

"Oh, Bear's taking Stetson to see the horses, as if he's never seen one before." She sounded cross, but she wore adoration in her expression. "And Mister took Russell for a minute. He was going to run home and get something, and I asked him to take the stroller. Russell will fall asleep in two seconds flat, and then I might be able to enjoy the party."

She gave Dawna a smile, and Dawna returned it. "Still going with Smiles for Stetson?"

"I'm trying," Sammy said. "It fits him, but I have a hard time letting it come out of my mouth."

"It'll grow on you," she said. "Just like Rock will for Russell."

"I actually like Rock," Sammy said. "Oh, there's Lois. I have to go ask her something. Excuse me."

"Of course," Dawna said, waving her hand. "Go." But Sammy was already gone.

Dawna smiled out at everyone at the party. All of the cowboys had come tonight, and someone had set up the speaker system to blast music into the sky. It wasn't dark yet, and wouldn't be for another couple of hours.

She loved her bird's eye view of the Glover family, in all their shapes, sizes, and personalities. "You would love it here so much," she whispered to Bull. "You would be so proud of them."

She was—each and every one of them.

"All right," Ranger called, and the music cut off. He took the mic from Ward and repeated, "All right," into it. "We're going to go ahead and get started. First, Oakley and I have an announcement." He looked at his beautiful wife, the perfect complement to him, and took her hand in his. "We're due with another baby in November."

Cheers, whoops, and applause filled the sky. Ranger and Oakley beamed out at everyone, and Dawna had never felt such happiness in her life. "Maybe the day I married you, Bull."

Definitely that day.

"Okay, okay," Ranger said, holding up his free hand to get everyone to quiet down. "Second, thanks to all the men and women who went out on the drive this year. It takes all of us to keep this ranch running smoothly." He twisted, and asked, "Where'd Bear get to?"

"Right here," Bear said, and the crowd parted for him. Bear had always been a mighty spirit in a tiny body. Now, his body was bigger, but his spirit had grown too. Everyone looked to him for guidance and direction, and he bore the burden well.

He arrived at Ranger's side and took the mic. "To echo Ranger, thank you," he said. "Stetson and I just put early summer bonuses in your boxes in the main stable, so be sure to check those before you go home."

"Yeehaw!" one of the cowboys yelled. Laughter followed, including from Bear and Ranger—and that was saying something.

Dawna smiled at the two of them standing shoulder-to-shoulder. Running this ranch. Becoming dedicated husbands and brilliant fathers. They kept the Glover family mottos, and they strove to love God, love the land, work hard, and move forward with faith.

Dawna's life felt complete in that moment, and she closed her eyes and wished the Lord would take her home while she felt so good.

"Yes," she whispered to her beloved Bull, who just had

to be somewhere close by listening. "You'd definitely be so proud of what they've done here at Shiloh Ridge."

Read on for a sneak peek at **THE NETWORKING OF THE NATIVITY**, which features Juniper Nichols and Judge Glover. Can they finally make a relationship into something meaningful and lasting after all these years?

Sneak Peek! The Networking of the Nativity, Chapter One:

J udge Glover put the last bite of his scrambled eggs in his mouth just as the door that led into the garage opened. Out of the two men he lived with—his cousin Ward and his brother Mister—he'd prefer it to be Ward.

He'd been getting along just fine with Mister since they'd made up several months ago. The younger man annoyed Judge from time to time—or all the time lately—but he kept his mouth shut.

He didn't tease his brother the way he would've in the past. He didn't play tricks on him—or anyone—anymore. It had taken him an extra-long time to mature, but he'd done it.

Mister walked in, a sour look on his face. Instant annoyance sprouted inside Judge. Still, he said, "Morning," and got up to wash the ketchup off his plate. Mister had said plenty of things over the years about how Judge ruined perfectly good eggs by putting ketchup on them.

He washed the red stuff down the drain and bent to put his plate in the dishwasher. He noted that Mister had not done that with his dishes that morning, and another dose of annoyance washed through him.

"Is June coming to Ward's wedding with you?" Mister asked, the chair scraping as he pulled it out from under the table. He sat in it with a big sigh. "I don't want to be the only one at the wedding without a date."

"I honestly don't know," Judge said, his mood only worsening with this topic of conversation. His relationship with June over the months could barely be categorized as such. She'd been called back to her house by her daughter and the police on their date after Christmas.

She hadn't been able to come to the impromptu New Year's Eve party they'd held at Shiloh Ridge Ranch, due to some previous plans she'd made with friends.

Judge hadn't given up there, but he probably should have. Days bled by, turning into weeks, and months, and while he sometimes talked to June on the phone, and they texted fairly regularly, he'd only seen her a few times.

He wasn't even sure he'd call running into her at the diner a date.

He'd asked her out a few times. She'd said yes. They'd made plans.

Something always came up—and not just on her end, so Judge didn't believe she was putting him off.

Lucy Mae had a band concert she hadn't put on the calendar. Judge had six calves born in the same day, so there was no way he could leave the ranch. June's car got hit in the parking lot, and she needed to take it to the body shop. Bear had called a family meeting after church, and Judge couldn't miss it. June had a massive system failure at her office in Oklahoma City, and she'd had to leave immediately to go fix it.

The list went on and on for what had gotten in the way of him taking her to dinner, going to her house after church, or the two of them simply getting together.

He was starting to think the Lord simply didn't want him to be with June. He'd backed off on texting and calling, and she hadn't made much effort to reach out to him either.

"Have you asked her to attend with you?" Mister pressed.

Judge cast him a glare, but the other man was staring at his phone. Probably looking through the long list of women's numbers he owned, trying to find someone he could ask to Ward's wedding. "Not exactly."

"Why not?" Mister looked up.

Judge turned back to the sink with a sigh. "Because, Mister, if I don't ask, then she can't tell me yes and then cancel later."

"At least she tells you yes," Mister grumbled as Judge picked up a butter knife. He contemplated stabbing it through his own eye, but just held it under the hot water and let the mayo melt off of it. He put it in the dishwasher as Mister continued, "Libby still refuses to tell me anything else about why she doesn't believe I like her. I've asked her out a couple of times, and she just says no."

"Maybe it's time to move on," Judge said, and he was telling himself as well as Mister.

"I don't want to move on."

"We don't always get what we want."

"Thanks, Dad," Mister said sarcastically.

"At least I don't," Judge said as if Mister hadn't even spoken. His chest vibrated in a strange way, and something told him not to say another word. "You seem to though."

The chair scraped again as Mister stood. "What does that mean?" He came closer to Judge, who twisted away from him to put a rinsed plate in the dishwasher. Probably Mister's, but who was keeping track?

Judge was, that was who.

"It doesn't mean anything."

"Yes, it does," Mister said. "If you have something to say, just say it."

Judge paused, cocked his head to the side, and flew backward in time to another argument they'd had. He'd lost his temper; Mister had too. Cruel things were said. Judge wasn't going to do that again.

"I'm sorry," he said slowly. "I shouldn't have said that." He met Mister's eye, noting the darkness and unhappiness there. His heart ached for his brother, because Judge knew what bitter feelings came with unhappiness. He and Preacher had talked about how to help Mister, but they'd come to no conclusions or solutions yet.

"It means something," Mister pressed, and he was never one to let anything go. That was why he couldn't just let Libby walk out of his life, despite her rejections. He'd gotten one kiss, a while ago, after he'd successfully sold an article she'd helped him edit to *Modern Rodeo*.

Since then, Mister hadn't been able to let go of Libby, no matter what anyone said. No matter that she'd broken their dinner date and then refused to go out with him. She'd said she just wanted to be friends, and that rejection had almost killed Mister.

Judge had been rejected too, and it was never pleasant. "I just...I don't want to hurt your feelings. It doesn't really matter what I think."

Mister nodded, his expression softening. "Will you tell me anyway?"

Judge paused, only the sound of the hot water running between them. "What if it upsets you?"

"I'm already upset," Mister said. "What's one more thing?"

He did seem to walk around in a perpetual bad mood lately. Maybe since New Year's, when everything with Libby blew up.

"I think you missed out on learning some things when you were younger," Judge said, trying to be delicate. He kept his voice low and his eyes trained on the mugs in the sink. Dark liquid spilled from them when he turned them over, and he rinsed them out. "Because you didn't have to go live in the cowboy cabin for a year, and you never had to work the ranch like a regular cowboy."

"I work the ranch just fine," Mister said, his default always defensive.

"I didn't say you didn't work hard," Judge said.

The door opened again, and Judge prayed it would be

Ward. Preacher walked in, and that was ten times better than Ward. He was the perfect buffer between Judge and Mister, and he paused instantly. "What's goin' on?" he asked, looking between the two of them.

"Nothing," Judge said, reaching to turn off the water.

"Judge was just telling me how lazy I am."

"That is *not* true," Judge said. "At all."

"What did you say?" Preacher asked, his eyes still zipping from brother to brother.

"I said he missed out on learning some lessons because he went straight into the rodeo. The rest of us had to go live in the cowboy cabins, draw the cowboy's daily wage, and learn how other people live and work." He glared at Mister. "That's what you don't get. Not everything goes your way all the time. I learned that while sharing a cabin with three other men and barely having enough money to pay for groceries." He drew a deep breath. "Or waiting for the shower, only to find out there was no hot water left for me."

"It was a tough time," Preacher said, committing to entering the house. "What do you guys have to eat here? We haven't been to the store in a while, and Charlie's promised to bring you back whatever you want." He smiled at Judge and hugged him quickly.

Judge hugged him back and watched as he stepped over to Mister too. Mister stood unyieldingly in his arms, his frown still pinned on Judge.

"There's bagels and cream cheese," Judge said, moving back to the table to get his coffee mug. He started rinsing that too.

"What other kinds of lessons?" Mister asked.

Judge sighed and looked up to the ceiling, wishing he could see all the way to heaven. He needed some help from On High right now, that was for sure.

"Patience, for one," Judge said. "And for two, you have no idea how regular people live. What they have to deal with."

"I'm a regular person," Mister said.

"No," Judge said with a laugh. "You're not. We're not. None of us up here are. You learn that in the cabins."

Mister looked at Preacher, who set two halves of his bagel into the toaster. "What does he mean?"

"The fact that you don't know is how I know you don't get why Libby won't go out with you."

"Is this about Libby?" Preacher asked.

"It's always about Libby," Judge said, and a bit of sarcasm crept into his voice. He cleared his throat to tame it. He wasn't going to poke fun at Mister for his crush on Liberty Bellamore. He wasn't, because that was cruel, and not what brothers should do to one another.

"Mister," Preacher said, turning toward him. "He's right, bro. We're not normal."

"In what way?"

"In the billion-dollar way," Preacher said. "In the way that if we want a new house, we just build it. We don't have to get a loan. We don't have to worry about making mortgage payments. We don't worry about anything, really. At least not when it comes to how things will get paid for. Things like medical expenses or new cars or...whatever."

"That's not how normal people live," Judge said gently.

"They have more bills than money. They have to decide if they should pay their electric bill or the prom dress their daughter wants. Sometimes it's medical care or groceries. I learned that in the cowboy cabins. I met men who were desperately trying to provide for themselves or a family."

"You think I got off easy." Mister folded his arms and glared.

"You did," Preacher and Judge said together. They exchanged a glance, and Preacher's jaw tightened. Judge had seen that look before, and he knew Preacher was done talking. Judge should be too.

"You learn to lean on yourself," Judge said quietly. "Or the Lord, even though Dad is just a few steps away. That's what he wanted us to learn." Judge had learned it too.

"You think I'm spoiled," Mister said.

"You have a lot of money, and a lot of shiny belt buckles, and a lot of titles," Judge said.

Mister folded his arms and glared. "Do you think I never had to lean on anyone while traveling the rodeo circuit by myself?" He threw his arms up. "Because that was no picnic, Judge. I was alone all the time. There's *so* much pressure out there."

"I think it's different," Judge said. "Out here, when it's just you, and you have nothing? You have no idea what that's like. You've been privileged your whole life, even while on the rodeo circuit." He pointed toward the door, toward the whole ranch. "Those men we employ? That's all they have. They don't have big bank accounts waiting for them at home or glitzy belt buckles. You walk around here like you own the world, and that's fine. You're a great guy, and you help others. I'm just saying...."

"What?" Mister demanded, dropping his arms and clenching his fists. "What are you saying?"

"I'm saying you're hard to relate to," Judge said, committed now. He swallowed and glanced at Preacher, who seemed to need to stare unblinkingly at his bagel while he spread cream cheese on it.

"It's no wonder Libby thinks you don't get it. You don't. You've been spoiled rotten your whole life. You work, but you don't have to, and you know it. For some of us, we had to live and breathe and work like a cowboy for a year, and all we got was the twenty grand."

"You knew you'd have a big bank account afterward," Mister said with a scoff. "Don't give me that."

"Okay," Judge said, holding up both hands. "I'm not going to argue with you about it anymore. I think you missed out on learning some really valuable life lessons. Stuff Dad and Uncle Bull *wanted* us to experience and learn. You never did, and in my opinion, it shows." He started for the front door, but he kept his steps slow and even. He wasn't mad. Mister could think what he wanted. Judge was just tired of listening to him moan and complain about how everything didn't go his way.

Welcome to the freaking club.

Judge had learned while living in a two-bedroom cabin with three other men that compromises could and should be made. He didn't have to get his way all the time. He could put his needs aside in favor of someone else's.

He'd learned to truly share—and not just his toys like

when he'd been a kid. But share parts of himself with other people. Share his resources so they could all have a good life. Share the workload so one of them wasn't left doing all the dirty dishes.

No, he didn't have the bejeweled belt buckles or the titles Mister did. But he had more wisdom and knowledge that actually helped him in the life he was trying to live now. He didn't complain that life got in the way of him and June being together. Life did that sometimes. It happened, and it didn't always go the way he wanted it to.

He knew his life was charmed too. He wasn't delirious or blind to that fact. But he had put himself in someone else's boots and walked and worked for a full year. Mister never had.

His life had been, and still was, all about *him*. What he wanted. What he didn't have. Why Libby wouldn't go out with him.

"I'm gonna go get started with the horses in six," he said. "Is that where you want me, boss?"

"I'm not your boss," Preacher said.

"But you are," Judge said. "I know you and Ward are the boss, and that's another thing I learned in the cowboy cabins. The work is hard, and it never ends, and the boss tells you what to do, and you do it."

Judge actually didn't mind that. He knew who he was, and it wasn't to be Preacher or Ward. He'd never survive as a leader the way they did. He didn't like all the pressure on him when tough decisions needed to be made.

He could work like a dog, and he often had around the ranch. He had around other ranches when their owners needed help. Judge liked to work. He just didn't want to be in charge.

"I follow orders too," Mister said.

"I'm not saying you don't," Judge said. "I'm saying I don't think you have any idea what it means to bend your will to someone else's. After all, you're *still* asking Libby out, and she's still telling you no."

"You are?" Preacher asked. "Didn't she tell you no like six months ago?"

"The horses in six?" Judge asked.

"Yep," Preacher said, and Judge reached for the door-knob. He yanked the door open and stepped outside—and right into someone standing there, their hand reaching for the doorbell.

Their fingers hit his shoulder, and he grunted at the same time the woman there yelped. He reached out and grabbed onto her so he wouldn't knock her down, and that was when Judge looked into the gorgeous, brown eyes of Juniper Nichols.

In the flesh.

His heart leapt to the back of his throat. "June," he gasped out, his hands moving down her arms and settling on her waist. He looked over his shoulder, quickly drop-ping his hands from her body so he could close the door.

He faced her, noting the nerves—and tears?—in her eyes now. "What are you doing here? Is everything okay?"

Sneak Peek! The Networking of the Nativity, Chapter Two:

Juniper Nichols told herself to *be cool. Play everything so cool.* In reality, she was hot under the collar, with burning tears behind her eyes.

"You look upset, June," Judge said. "What can I help you with?"

"I was just down the lane at Ace's," she said, stepping with him as he pressed her toward the edge of the porch. This one only had three steps leading to it, and it was clearly decades older than the house she'd just visited. "They needed some help with their WiFI. I got them a new cord, and they're good as new."

"Great," he said with a smile. "I'm headed over to the stables. Do you have a minute to walk with me?"

"No," she said, and Judge continued down the steps before he turned back to her. "I just heard that Ward is getting married this weekend. Holly Ann was on the phone with someone."

"Yes," Judge said, looking toward the homestead. That house dwarfed this one, though where Judge lived was twice as big as what June had.

"Why didn't you ask me to go with you?" June went down the steps too, and when she reached Judge, she laced her arm through his. "Can I go with you?" Her voice broke on the last word, drawing the cowboy's attention.

"Can you come with me to the wedding?" he asked. "Of course you can come with me." He leaned down and touched his lips to her forehead. "I didn't ask you, because I was afraid you'd say yes, and then cancel on me."

Instant defenses flew into place. "I didn't cancel any of the times because I didn't want to go out with you."

"I know that."

"You canceled on me too."

"I know that."

June let the morning silence settle over them. "Life has been really funny the past six months."

"Yes, it has." Judge tucked her arm closer to his body. "Plus, I don't believe you didn't know about Ward's wedding. You're on that text with all the women." He looked at her, his eyebrows cocked.

June's emotions stormed through her like an army of soldiers. "Actually, I asked Willa to remove me," she whispered. "It was too hard, knowing all the amazing stuff they were doing together and not being able to do any of it. I didn't...I don't...I don't belong with them."

"You could," he said.

"Judge Glover," June said, a smile dancing across her face. "You best not be sayin' things you don't mean."

He started to laugh, and June joined him. "It's been an interesting ride with you, Juniper."

She liked it when he used her full name, and she'd hated her full name since grade school. Somehow, when Judge said it, it became a term of endearment.

He drew in a deep breath. "I also didn't ask, because I know Lucy Mae graduates on Friday. I believe you told me she was leaving for California the next day—and that's the day Ward is getting married."

Those pesky tears entered her eyes again. She knew if she spoke, Judge would hear them. He'd look at her and see them again. "Yes," she said anyway, and he did exactly what she feared he would.

She let him look, and she let him see, and he did exactly what she hoped he would. He gathered her close to his chest, enveloping her in his strong arms, and whispered, "It's okay, June-Bug. It's all going to be okay."

She pressed her eyes closed, because her only daughter leaving Three Rivers wasn't okay. Such a thing wasn't even in the same realm as okay. "I don't know how to be alone," she said.

"Maybe you won't have to be," he said.

"I don't know how to have enough faith that she'll be okay in California."

"Maybe I can help," he said.

June pulled away slightly and looked up at him. "Why won't you go out with anyone else?"

"Have you?" he asked.

She shook her head. "I sort of have a policy about that."

"Yeah, but you'll break that policy for the right guy," Judge said, dead serious. "Right?"

"I guess."

"Have you been asked out in the past six months?"

"Yes," she said.

"By someone other than me?"

"Yes."

Judge frowned, and he obviously didn't like that. "Did you say yes?"

"No." A relationship with him felt impossible. It was exactly as she'd told Ida a couple of months ago. Maybe God simply didn't want June to have someone as amazing as Judge in her life.

"I don't want to ask you to come to the wedding," he said. "If you're available and you want to come, that's fine. No one's going to turn you away." He stepped gently away from her, and they both looked up to the door when it opened again.

Preacher came outside, and he paused, surprise evident on his face. "Hey, uh, when you're done here, can I talk to you for a sec?"

"Sure," Judge said, looking from his brother to June. "I think we're done. Miss Nichols surely has a full schedule today to be at the ranch so early." He reached up and tipped his hat to her, his smile gorgeous and perfectly symmetrical, with all those shiny, white teeth.

She watched him go up the few steps and say, "What's up? I overstepped with Mister, didn't I?" before the two of them went inside and the door closed behind them. She knew Judge and Mister didn't always get along, and she wanted to know what boundary he'd overstepped.

She wanted him at her side this summer while Lucy Mae was gone. She'd wanted more of a relationship with him the past few months, but she'd let the tides of life push her this way and then that one.

She wanted to see his Christmas display, and help him upgrade his network to make it run flawlessly.

She wanted to tell him that Adam was coming to pick up Lucy Mae, and she was scared out of her mind to see her ex-husband for the first time in thirteen years. She'd spoken to him when she'd had to, but she hadn't been in the same physical space as him since he'd left her and Lucy Mae all those years ago.

While still standing on the front sidewalk in front of Bull House, she sent a text to Judge. *Can you go to dinner tonight? I'll be done by five-thirty, and I have something I want to tell you.*

Sure, he said almost instantly, and she could hear it in his cowboy twang. The man said "Sure," as easily as he breathed, and with a date with him on the horizon, June finally felt like *she* could breathe again.

"DID YOU GET YOUR CAP AND GOWN?" JUNE ASKED WHEN her daughter walked in from her after school job. She pulled the pan of lasagna from the oven. "Dinner's almost ready."

"I'm going out with Timmy tonight, remember?" Lucy

Mae dropped her backpack by the door and kicked off her shoes. "Yes, I got my cap and gown. You would not believe how many cars came through the line today." She smiled and reached for one of the caramels June had gotten out for herself.

"I forgot about Timmy." June frowned and looked at the pan of lasagna. She wouldn't have made it if she'd remembered. After all, she had a dinner date tonight too.

Maybe Judge could just come here, she thought, and she reached for her phone as Lucy Mae filled a glass with water.

"And some of them went through the line twice, saying we had to give them a free wash, because the first one didn't get the mud off."

"What are you and Timmy doing?"

"I argued with this one guy until Gerome came out and said to just give it to him." She shook her head and took a big drink. "But honestly, the entire town got the mud rained on them. It's all over everything, from the garbage cans to the fence posts. I should work on tips." She grinned, and June smiled back at her.

Lucy Mae had always been a talker, and she could go on and on—and on—about almost anything. When she'd been obsessed with Broadway, June had listened to the plot of every play Lucy Mae could get her hands on. And not a short synopsis either.

"Timmy's taking me to the senior hot dog roast," she said. "Tomorrow is the all-nighter."

"I don't want you out all night."

"I know, Mom. We already talked about it." Lucy Mae

rolled her eyes and put her glass in the sink. "Sorry about the lasagna. We'll eat it, I'm sure."

"I'm thinking of having Judge come help." She looked from the Italian dish to her daughter.

Lucy Mae's eyebrows soared toward the ceiling "Judge Glover? I thought you'd decided to let life play its course, and he wasn't included."

"Maybe he still is," June said. "I saw him today."

"Where?"

"The ranch. I had a job up there."

Lucy Mae cocked one hip and put her hand on it. "Did you, Mom? Or did you go seek him out?"

"What if I did?" she asked. "People can alter their course in life, you know." She put the oven mitts back in the drawer next to the stove. "I'm letting you go to California, and that's a complete life course deviation." She gave her daughter a glare, not wanting to admit how much she still liked and thought about Judge Glover.

"I will text you every hour," Lucy Mae said.

June scoffed, caught her daughter's grin, and drew her into a hug. "I love you so much, Lucy Mae."

"I love you too, Mom."

"I can't believe you're graduating and moving out. Moving on. You're going to have such an amazing life." She stepped back, used to letting her daughter see her tears. She didn't let them slip down her face, but they definitely brimmed in her eyes.

"So are you," Lucy Mae said. "You'll finally be free to do what you want."

"You have never been a burden to me," June said firmly. "Never."

"I know." Lucy Mae hugged her again, and June felt something extra in the touch. Her daughter held her tighter, and June did the same in return.

They stepped apart, and Lucy Mae wiped her eyes. "I'm going to go shower. If Timmy gets here before I'm done, please be nice to him."

"I'm always nice to him," June said.

"Mom, last time you told him you could find out where he'd been on the Internet. 'Two clicks, Timmy, and that history is mine.' That's what you said." Lucy Mae rolled her eyes again, but June only smiled.

She knew better than most the dangers out there on the Internet, and she knew about the enticing things that teenage boys could get into.

Her daughter went down the hall to her bathroom, and June muttered, "That *was* me being nice, baby." She knew the ins and outs of routers, networks, security systems, and backend servers. She could sit outside Timmy's house and, within five minutes, be spying on what he was doing on his computer.

She wouldn't, of course. But she could.

She picked up her phone and called Judge, hoping he wasn't up to his elbows in manure or something. Now that summer had arrived, Judge would be pulling his Christmas supplies out of the basement, and the more likely scenario would have him wrapped up in old strings of Christmas lights.

"Heya, June," he said, and it sounded like he was

running. "Can I call you back in maybe ten minutes?"

"Sure," she said quickly, and he said, "Great, thanks," and the call ended.

June smiled to herself, because it sure felt like Judge would provide a life for her that would never have a dull moment. She looked around her house, feeling very much like a boring, old maid.

She needed some excitement in her life—and not the kind where her entire Oklahoma City office was offline.

But the cowboy kind.

The *sexy* cowboy kind, and she grabbed her phone and went down the hall to her bedroom and bathroom. If Judge was coming over, she needed to freshen up a little bit. She caught sight of herself in the mirror and gasped.

The manly polo with *Nichols Networking* stitched over the breast came right off. "I need new company shirts," she muttered to herself. Something with a V-neck or something that didn't make her look so boxy.

She stepped out of her work boots and pants and slipped into some black slacks made of something silky.

"Mom?" Lucy Mae called.

"I'm changing," she said, turning her back toward the door, as her daughter would come in whether she was changing or not. She searched her limited closet space for something appropriate for a date in her own home.

She glanced at her daughter as she entered the closet. She must've been able to read June's mind, because Lucy Mae said, "You want something to bring out your eyes." She stepped over to the rack and started flipping. "And since it's the beginning of summer, and you're a little pale from winter, you want—"

"I am not pale from winter," June said. "The sun's been shining in Texas for months."

"Something blue or purple, I think," Lucy Mae continued, not bothered at all by June's protest. She plucked a purple blouse from the options and held it up. "This one's really cute."

The blouse had little white confetti blotches all over it, and June reached out to touch the material. It was light and airy, and June would feel confident in it. "Okay," she said, taking the blouse off the hanger. She pulled it over her head and then took the ponytail holder out of her hair.

"Up or down?"

"Down, Mom. Always down when you're trying to impress a man."

June's lungs seized. "I've always had it up when I've seen him before."

Lucy Mae smiled and reached over to fluff June's hair. "Then he'll be doubly impressed tonight."

"Yeah, the way I heated up that frozen lasagna is going to win him over for good."

Lucy Mae giggled and kept arranging June's hair. "Looks good now. Come and let me do your makeup."

"I don't want a lot of makeup."

"I'll choose three things," Lucy Mae said. "I won't do a single thing more." She opened the top drawer in June's vanity and started digging through her makeup bag. "Mascara, foundation, and lip gloss." She held them up, and the makeup looked so innocent. "Doable?"

"Doable," June said, and she followed Lucy Mae back into the kitchen. She sat at the dining room table, and she closed her eyes and let her daughter start to paint her face.

The doorbell rang, and Lucy Mae left quickly to go answer it. As she greeted her boyfriend, June's phone rang. Judge's name sat on the screen, and she hurried to answer the call.

"Hey," she said. "You really called back."

"I was chasing a turkey, believe it or not," he said with a laugh. "Stupid thing got into some cord, and we needed to get it off his feet."

"Sounds exciting," she said. "I didn't know you had turkeys."

"We have a little bit of everything up here," he said with a sigh. "Let me guess—something came up?"

"Yes," June said, grinning to herself and then looking at Lucy Mae and Timmy as they came into the kitchen. "I forgot my daughter had a date tonight, and I made dinner for her so we could go out and I wouldn't feel guilty. I'm wondering if you'd like to come to my place to eat instead of going out."

"Absolutely," Judge said. "I'm headed home now, so I just need to shower and make the drive. Say, an hour?"

"Can't wait," June said, hoping she'd used a flirtatious voice.

"Wow, Mom," Lucy Mae said as Judge said good-bye, and June hung up.

"What?" she asked. "You can't leave until you finish my makeup."

"Can't wait," Lucy Mae said in a falsely high voice, a

poor imitation of June. She giggled and waved with the mascara wand. "Eyes closed. I'm going to make your face match that flirty tone, and you're going to show this cowboy he shouldn't let a day go by without talking to you."

"From your lips to God's ears," June sad, immediately following that up with a silent prayer that the Lord would indeed help her with her at-home dinner date with Judge Glover in only an hour.

Read now!

The Mechanics of Mistletoe (Book 1): Bear Glover can be a grizzly or a teddy, and he's always thought he'd be just fine working his generational family ranch and going back to the ancient homestead alone. But his crush on Samantha Benton won't go away. She's a genius with a wrench on Bear's tractors...and his heart. Can he tame his wild side and get the girl, or will he be left broken-hearted this Christmas season?

The Horsepower of the Holiday (Book 2): Ranger Glover has worked at Shiloh Ridge Ranch his entire life. The cowboys do everything from horseback there, but when he goes to town to trade in some trucks, somehow Oakley Hatch persuades him to take some ATVs back to the ranch. (Bear is NOT happy.)

She's a former race car driver who's got Ranger all revved up... Can he remember who he is and get Oakley to slow down enough to fall in love, or will there simply be too much horsepower in the holiday this year for a real relationship?

The Construction of Cheer (Book 3): Bishop Glover is the youngest brother, and he usually keeps his head down and gets the job done. When Montana Martin shows up at Shiloh Ridge Ranch looking for work, he finds himself inventing construction projects that need doing just to keep her coming around. (Again, Bear is NOT happy.) She wants to build her own construction firm, but she ends up carving a place for herself inside Bishop's heart. Can he convince her *he's* all she needs this Christmas season, or will her cheer rest solely on the success of her business?

The Secret of Santa (Book 4): He's a fun-loving cowboy with a heart of gold. She's the woman who keeps putting him on hold. Can Ace and Holly Ann make a relationship work this Christmas?

The Harmony of Holly (Book 5): He's as prickly as his name, but the new woman in town has caught his eye. Can Cactus shelve his temper and shed his cowboy hermit skin fast enough to make a relationship with Willa work?

The Chemistry of Christmas (Book 6): He's the black sheep of the family, and she's a chemist who understands formulas, not emotions. Can Preacher and Charlie take their quirks and turn them into a strong relationship this Christmas?

The Delivery of Decor (Book 7): When he falls, he falls hard and deep. She literally drives away from every relationship she's ever had. Can Ward somehow get Dot to stay this Christmas?

USA Today Bestselling Author
LIZ ISAACSON

The Blessing of Babies (Book 8): Don't miss out on a single moment of the Glover family saga in this bridge story linking Ward and Judge's love stories!

The Glovers love God, country, dogs, horses, and family. Not necessarily in that order. ;)

Many of them are married now, with babies on the way, and there are lessons to be learned, forgiveness to be had and given, and new names coming to the family tree in southern Three Rivers!

The Networking of the Nativity (Book 9): He's had a crush on her for years. She doesn't want to date until her daughter is out of the house. Will June take a change on Judge when the success of his Christmas light display depends on her networking abilities?

CHRISTMAS AT SHILOH RIDGE RANCH

The
WRANGLING
of the Wreath

USA Today Bestselling Author
LIZ ISAACSON

The Wrangling of the Wreath (Book 10): He's been so busy trying to find Miss Right. She's been right in front of him the whole time. This Christmas, can Mister and Libby take their relationship out of the best friend zone?

The Hope of Her Heart (Book 11): She's the only Glover without a significant other. He's been searching for someone who can love him *and* his daughter. Can Etta and August make a meaningful connection this Christmas?

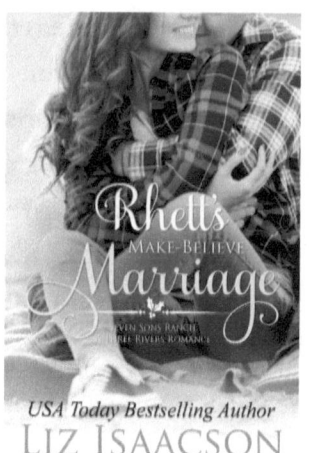

Rhett's Make-Believe Marriage (Book 1): She needs a husband to be credible as a matchmaker. He wants to help a neighbor. Will their fake marriage take them out of the friend zone?

Tripp's Trivial Tie (Book 2): She needs a husband to keep her son. He's wanted to take their relationship to the next level, but she's always pushing him away. Will their trivial tie take them all the way to happily-ever-after?

USA Today Bestselling Author
LIZ ISAACSON

Liam's Invented I-Do (Book 3): She's desperate to save her ranch. He wants to help her any way he can. Will their invented I-Do open doors that have previously been closed and lead to a happily-ever-after for both of them?

Jeremiah's Bogus Bride (Book 4): He wants to prove to his brothers that he's not broken. She just wants him. Will a fake marriage heal him or push her further away?

USA Today Bestselling Author
LIZ ISAACSON

Wyatt's Pretend Pledge (Book 5): To get her inheritance, she needs a husband. He's wanted to fly with her for ages. Can their pretend pledge turn into something real?

Skyler's Wanna-Be Wife (Book 6): She needs a new last name to stay in school. He's willing to help a fellow student. Can this wanna-be wife show the playboy that some things should be taken seriously?

LIZ ISAACSON

Micah's Mock Matrimony (Book 7): They were just actors auditioning for a play. The marriage was just for the audition – until a clerical error results in a legal marriage. Can these two ex-lovers negotiate this new ground between them and achieve new roles in each other's lives?

Her Cowboy Billionaire Birthday Wish (Book 1): All the maid at Whiskey Mountain Lodge wants for her birthday is a handsome cowboy billionaire. And Colton can make that wish come true—if only he hadn't escaped to Coral Canyon after being left at the altar...

Her Cowboy Billionaire Butler (Book 2): She broke up with him to date another man...who broke her heart. He's a former CEO with nothing to do who can't get her out of his head. Can Wes and Bree find a way toward happily-ever-after at Whiskey Mountain Lodge?

Her Cowboy Billionaire Best Friend's Brother (Book 3): She's best friends with the single dad cowboy's brother and has watched two friends find love with the sexy new cowboys in town. When Gray Hammond comes to Whiskey Mountain Lodge with his son, will Elise finally get her own happily-ever-after with one of the Hammond brothers?

Her Cowboy Billionaire Beast (Book 4): A cowboy billionaire beast, his new manager, and the Christmas traditions that soften his heart and bring them together.

Her Cowboy Billionaire Bad Boy (Book 5): A cowboy billionaire cop who's a stickler for rules, the woman he pulls over when he's not even on duty, and the personal mandates he has to break to keep her in his life...

Books in the Christmas in Coral Canyon Romance series

Her Cowboy Billionaire Best Friend (Book 1): Graham Whittaker returns to Coral Canyon a few days after Christmas—after the death of his father. He takes over the energy company his dad built from the ground up and buys a high-end lodge to live in—only a mile from the home of his once-best friend, Laney McAllister. They were best friends once, but Laney's always entertained feelings for him, and spending so much time with him while they make Christmas memories puts her heart in danger of getting broken again...

Her Cowboy Billionaire Boss (Book 2): Since the death of his wife a few years ago, Eli Whittaker has been running from one job to another, unable to find somewhere for him and his son to settle. Meg Palmer is Stockton's nanny, and she comes with her boss, Eli, to the lodge, her long-time crush on the man no different in Wyoming than it was on the beach. When she confesses her feelings for him and gets nothing in return, she's crushed, embarrassed, and unsure if she can stay in Coral Canyon for Christmas. Then Eli starts to show some feelings for her too...

Her Cowboy Billionaire Boyfriend (Book 3): Andrew Whittaker is the public face for the Whittaker Brothers' family energy company, and with his older brother's robot about to be announced, he needs a press secretary to help him get everything ready and tour the state to make the announcements. When he's hit by a protest sign being carried by the company's biggest opponent, Rebecca Collings, he learns with a few clicks that she has the background they need. He offers her the job of press secretary when she thought she was going to be arrested, and not only because the spark between them in so hot Andrew can't see straight.

Can Becca and Andrew work together and keep their relationship a secret? Or will hearts break in this classic romance retelling reminiscent of *Two Weeks Notice*?

Her Cowboy Billionaire Bodyguard (Book 4): Beau Whittaker has watched his brothers find love one by one, but every attempt he's made has ended in disaster. Lily Everett has been in the spotlight since childhood and has half a dozen platinum records with her two sisters. She's taking a break from the brutal music industry and hiding out in Wyoming while her ex-husband continues to cause trouble for her. When she hears of Beau Whittaker and what he offers his clients, she wants to meet him. Beau is instantly attracted to Lily, but he tried a relationship with his last client that left a scar that still hasn't healed...

Can Lily use the spirit of Christmas to discover what matters most? Will Beau open his heart to the possibility of love with someone so different from him?

Her Cowboy Billionaire Bull Rider (Book 5): Todd Christopherson has just retired from the professional rodeo circuit and returned to his hometown of Coral Canyon. Problem is, he's got no family there anymore, no land, and no job. Not that he needs a job--he's got plenty of money from his illustrious career riding bulls.

Then Todd gets thrown during a routine horseback ride up the canyon, and his only support as he recovers physically is the beautiful Violet Everett. She's no nurse, but she does the best she can for the handsome cowboy. **Will she lose her heart to the billionaire bull rider? Can Todd trust that God led him to Coral Canyon...and Vi?**

Her Cowboy Billionaire Bachelor (Book 6): Rose Everett isn't sure what to do with her life now that her country music career is on hold. After all, with both of her sisters in Coral Canyon, and one about to have a baby, they're not making albums anymore.

Liam Murphy has been working for Doctors Without Borders, but he's back in the US now, and looking to start a new clinic in Coral Canyon, where he spent his summers.

When Rose wins a date with Liam in a bachelor auction, their relationship blooms and grows quickly. **Can Liam and Rose find a solution to their problems that doesn't involve one of them leaving Coral Canyon with a broken heart?**

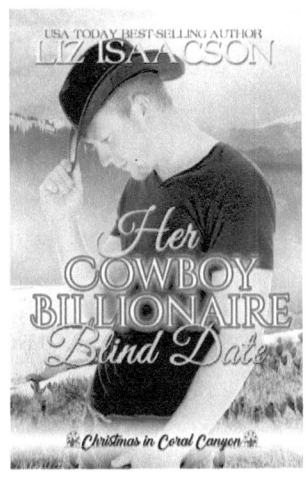

Her Cowboy Billionaire Blind Date (Book 7): Her sons want her to be happy, but she's too old to be set up on a blind date...isn't she?

Amanda Whittaker has been looking for a second chance at love since the death of her husband several years ago. Finley Barber is a cowboy in every sense of the word. Born and raised on a racehorse farm in Kentucky, he's since moved to Dog Valley and started his own breeding stable for champion horses. He hasn't dated in years, and everything about Amanda makes him nervous.

Will Amanda take the leap of faith required to be with Finn? Or will he become just another boyfriend who doesn't make the cut?

Her Cowboy Billionaire Best Man (Book 8): When Celia Abbott-Armstrong runs into a gorgeous cowboy at her best friend's wedding, she decides she's ready to start dating again.

But the cowboy is Zach Zuckerman, and the Zuckermans and Abbotts have been at war for generations.

Can Zach and Celia find a way to reconcile their family's differences so they can have a future together?

Second Chance Ranch: A Three Rivers Ranch Romance (Book 1): After his deployment, injured and discharged Major Squire Ackerman returns to Three Rivers Ranch, wanting to forgive Kelly for ignoring him a decade ago. He'd like to provide the stable life she needs, but with old wounds opening and a ranch on the brink of financial collapse, it will take patience and faith to make their second chance possible.

Third Time's the Charm: A Three Rivers Ranch Romance (Book 2): First Lieutenant Peter Marshall has a truckload of debt and no way to provide for a family, but Chelsea helps him see past all the obstacles, all the scars. With so many unknowns, can Pete and Chelsea develop the love, acceptance, and faith needed to find their happily ever after?

Fourth and Long: A Three Rivers Ranch Romance (Book 3): Commander Brett Murphy goes to Three Rivers Ranch to find some rest and relaxation with his Army buddies. Having his ex-wife show up with a seven-year-old she claims is his son is anything but the R&R he craves. Kate needs to make amends, and Brett needs to find forgiveness, but are they too late to find their happily ever after?

Fifth Generation Cowboy: A Three Rivers Ranch Romance (Book 4): Tom Lovell has watched his friends find their true happiness on Three Rivers Ranch, but everywhere he looks, he only sees friends. Rose Reyes has been bringing her daughter out to the ranch for equine therapy for months, but it doesn't seem to be working. Her challenges with Mari are just as frustrating as ever. Could Tom be exactly what Rose needs? Can he remove his friendship blinders and find love with someone who's been right in front of him all this time?

LIZ ISAACSON

Sixth
Street
Love
Affair

A THREE RIVERS RANCH ROMANCE NOVELLA

Sixth Street Love Affair: A Three Rivers Ranch Romance (Book 5): After losing his wife a few years back, Garth Ahlstrom thinks he's ready for a second chance at love. But Juliette Thompson has a secret that could destroy their budding relationship. Can they find the strength, patience, and faith to make things work?

LIZ ISAACSON

The Seventh Sergeant: A Three Rivers Ranch Romance (Book 6): Life has finally started to settle down for Sergeant Reese Sanders after his devastating injury overseas. Discharged from the Army and now with a good job at Courage Reins, he's finally found happiness—until a horrific fall puts him right back where he was years ago: Injured and depressed. Carly Watters, Reese's new veteran care coordinator, dislikes small towns almost as much as she loathes cowboys. But she finds herself faced with both when she gets assigned to Reese's case. Do they have the humility and faith to make their relationship more than professional?

Eight Second Ride: A Three Rivers Ranch Romance (Book 7): Ethan Greene loves his work at Three Rivers Ranch, but he can't seem to find the right woman to settle down with. When sassy yet vulnerable Brynn Bowman shows up at the ranch to recruit him back to the rodeo circuit, he takes a different approach with the barrel racing champion. His patience and newfound faith pay off when a friendship--and more--starts with Brynn. But she wants out of the rodeo circuit right when Ethan wants to rejoin. Can they find the path God wants them to take and still stay together?

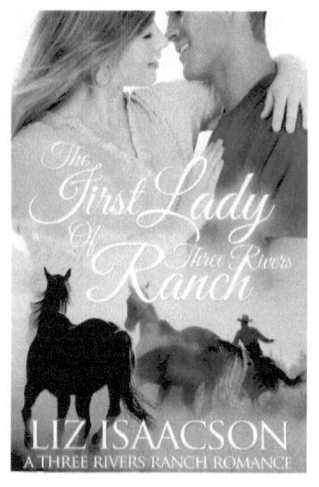

The First Lady of Three Rivers Ranch: A Three Rivers Ranch Romance (Book 8): Heidi Duffin has been dreaming about opening her own bakery since she was thirteen years old. She scrimped and saved for years to afford baking and pastry school in San Francisco. And now she only has one year left before she's a certified pastry chef. Frank Ackerman's father has recently retired, and he's taken over the largest cattle ranch in the Texas Panhandle. A horseman through and through, he's also nearing thirty-one and looking for someone to bring love and joy to a homestead that's been dominated by men for a decade. But when he convinces Heidi to come clean the cowboy cabins, she changes all that. But the siren's call of a bakery is still loud in Heidi's ears, even if she's also seeing a future with Frank. Can she rely on her faith in ways she's never had to before or will their relationship end when summer does?

Christmas in Three Rivers: A Three Rivers Ranch Romance (Book 9): Isn't Christmas the best time to fall in love? The cowboys of Three Rivers Ranch think so. Join four of them as they journey toward their path to happily ever after in four, all-new novellas in the Amazon #1 Bestselling Three Rivers Ranch Romance series.

THE NINTH INNING: The Christmas season has never felt like such a burden to boutique owner Andrea Larsen. But with Mama gone and the holidays upon her, Andy finds herself wishing she hadn't been so quick to judge her former boyfriend, cowboy Lawrence Collins. Well, Lawrence hasn't forgotten about Andy either, and he devises a plan to get her out to the ranch so they can reconnect. Do they have the faith and humility to patch things up and start a new relationship?

TEN DAYS IN TOWN: Sandy Keller is tired of the dating scene in Three Rivers. Though she owns the pancake house, she's looking for a fresh start, which means an escape from the town where she grew up. When her older brother's best friend, Tad Jorgensen, comes to town for the holidays, it is a balm to his weary soul. A helicopter tour guide who experienced a near-death experience, he's looking to start over too--but in Three Rivers. Can Sandy and Tad navigate their troubles to find the path God wants them to take--and discover true love--in only ten days?

ELEVEN YEAR REUNION: Pastry chef extraordinaire, Grace Lewis has moved to Three Rivers to help Heidi Ackerman open a bakery in Three Rivers. Grace relishes the idea of starting over in a town where no one knows about her failed cupcakery. She doesn't expect to run into her old high school boyfriend, Jonathan Carver. A carpenter working at Three Rivers Ranch, Jon's in town against his will. But with Grace now on the scene, Jon's thinking life in Three Rivers is suddenly looking up. But with her focus on baking and his disdain for small towns, can they make their eleven year reunion stick?

THE TWELFTH TOWN: Newscaster Taryn Tucker has had enough of life on-screen. She's bounced from town to town before arriving in Three Rivers, completely alone and completely anonymous--just the way she now likes it. She takes a job cleaning at Three Rivers Ranch, hoping for a chance to figure out who she is and where God wants her. When she meets happy-go-lucky cowhand Kenny Stockton, she doesn't expect sparks to fly. Kenny's always been "the best friend" for his female friends, but the pull between him and Taryn can't be denied. Will they have the courage and faith necessary to make their opposite worlds mesh?

Lucky Number Thirteen: A Three Rivers Ranch Romance (Book 10): Tanner Wolf, a rodeo champion ten times over, is excited to be riding in Three Rivers for the first time since he left his philandering ways and found religion. Seeing his old friends Ethan and Brynn is thera-puetic--until a terrible accident lands him in the hospital. With his rodeo career over, Tanner thinks maybe he'll stay in town--and it's not just because his nurse, Summer Hamblin, is the prettiest woman he's ever met. But Summer's the queen of first dates, and as she looks for a way to make a relationship with the transient rodeo star work Summer's not sure she has the fortitude to go on a second date. Can they find love among the tragedy?

The Curse of February Fourteenth: A Three Rivers Ranch Romance (Book 11): Cal Hodgkins, cowboy veterinarian at Bowman's Breeds, isn't planning to meet anyone at the masked dance in small-town Three Rivers. He just wants to get his bachelor friends off his back and sit on the sidelines to drink his punch. But when he sees a woman dressed in gorgeous butterfly wings and cowgirl boots with blue stitching, he's smitten. Too bad she runs away from the dance before he can get her name, leaving only her boot behind...

Fifteen Minutes of Fame: A Three Rivers Ranch Romance (Book 12): Navy Richards is thirty-five years of tired—tired of dating the same men, working a demanding job, and getting her heart broken over and over again. Her aunt has always spoken highly of the matchmaker in Three Rivers, Texas, so she takes a six-month sabbatical from her high-stress job as a pediatric nurse, hops on a bus, and meets with the matchmaker. Then she meets Gavin Redd. He's handsome, he's hardworking, and he's a cowboy. But is he an Aquarius too? Navy's not making a move until she knows for sure...

Sixteen Steps to Fall in Love: A Three Rivers Ranch Romance (Book 13): A chance encounter at a dog park sheds new light on the tall, talented Boone that Nicole can't ignore. As they get to know each other better and start to dig into each other's past, Nicole is the one who wants to run. This time from her growing admiration and attachment to Boone. From her aging parents. From herself.

But Boone feels the attraction between them too, and he decides he's tired of running and ready to make Three Rivers his permanent home. **Can Boone and Nicole use their faith to overcome their differences and find a happily-ever-after together?**

The Sleigh on Seventeenth Street: A Three Rivers Ranch Romance (Book 14): A cowboy with skills as an electrician tries a relationship with a down-on-her luck plumber. Can Dylan and Camila make water and electricity play nicely together this Christmas season? Or will they get shocked as they try to make their relationship work?

Books in the Last Chance Ranch Romance series

Last Chance Ranch (Book 1): A cowgirl down on her luck hires a man who's good with horses and under the hood of a car. Can Hudson fine tune Scarlett's heart as they work together? Or will things backfire and make everything worse at Last Chance Ranch?

Last Chance Cowboy (Book 2): A billionaire cowboy without a home meets a woman who secretly makes food videos to pay her debts...Can Carson and Adele do more than fight in the kitchens at Last Chance Ranch?

Last Chance Wedding (Book 3): A female carpenter needs a husband just for a few days... Can Jeri and Sawyer navigate the minefield of a pretend marriage before their feelings become real?

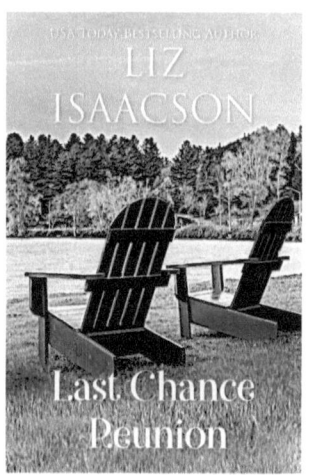

Last Chance Reunion (Book 4): An Army cowboy, the woman he dated years ago, and their last chance at Last Chance Ranch... Can Dave and Sissy put aside hurt feelings and make their second chance romance work?

Last Chance Lake (Book 5):
A former dairy farmer and the marketing director on the ranch have to work together to make the cow cuddling program a success. But can Karla let Cache into her life? Or will she keep all her secrets from him - and keep *him* a secret too?

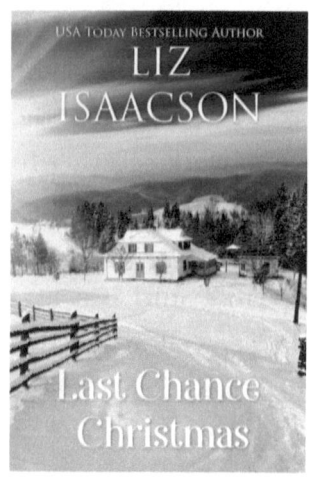

Last Chance Christmas (Book 6): She's tired of having her heart broken by cowboys. He waited too long to ask her out. Can Lance fix things quickly, or will Amber leave Last Chance Ranch before he can tell her how he feels?

Books in the Steeple Ridge Romance Series:

Her Billionaire Cowboy (Book 1): Tucker Jenkins has had enough of tall buildings, traffic, and has traded in his technology firm in New York City for Steeple Ridge Horse Farm in rural Vermont. Missy Marino has worked at the farm since she was a teen, and she's always dreamed of owning it. But her ex-husband left her with a truckload of debt, making her fantasies of owning the farm unfulfilled. Tucker didn't come to the country to find a new wife, but he supposes a woman could help him start over in Steeple Ridge. Will Tucker and Missy be able to navigate the shaky ground between them to find a new beginning?

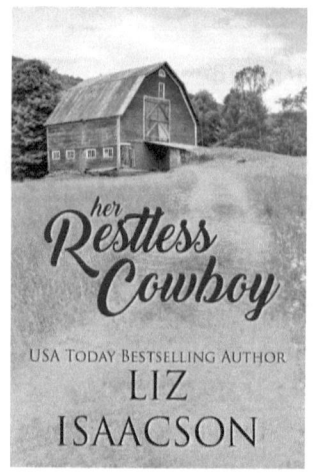

Her Restless Cowboy: A Butters Brothers Novel, Steeple Ridge Romance (Book 2): Ben Buttars is the youngest of the four Buttars brothers who come to Steeple Ridge Farm, and he finally feels like he's landed somewhere he can make a life for himself. Reagan Cantwell is a decade older than Ben and the recreational direction for the town of Island Park. Though Ben is young, he knows what he wants—and that's Rae. Can she figure out how to put what matters most in her life—family and faith—above her job before she loses Ben?

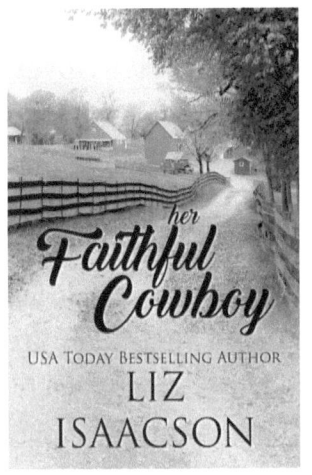

Her Faithful Cowboy: A Butters Brothers Novel, Steeple Ridge Romance (Book 3): Sam Buttars has spent the last decade making sure he and his brothers stay together. They've been at Steeple Ridge for a while now, but with the youngest married and happy, the siren's call to return to his parents' farm in Wyoming is loud in Sam's ears. He'd just go if it weren't for beautiful Bonnie Sherman, who roped his heart the first time he saw her. Do Sam and Bonnie have the faith to find comfort in each other instead of in the people who've already passed?

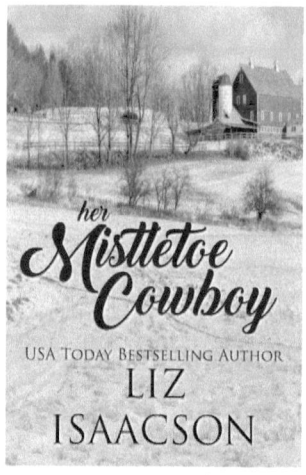

Her Mistletoe Cowboy: A Butters Brothers Novel, Steeple Ridge Romance (Book 4): Logan Buttars has always been good-natured and happy-go-lucky. After watching two of his brothers settle down, he recognizes a void in his life he didn't know about. Veterinarian Layla Guyman has appreciated Logan's friendship and easy way with animals when he comes into the clinic to get the service dogs. But with his future at Steeple Ridge in the balance, she's not sure a relationship with him is worth the risk. Can she rely on her faith and employ patience to tame Logan's wild heart?

USA TODAY BESTSELLING AUTHOR

LIZ ISAACSON

Her Patient Cowboy: A Butters Brothers Novel, Steeple Ridge Romance (Book 5): Darren Buttars is cool, collected, and quiet—and utterly devastated when his girl-friend of nine months, Farrah Irvine, breaks up with him because he wanted her to ride her horse in a parade. But Farrah doesn't ride anymore, a fact she made very clear to Darren. She returned to her childhood home with so much baggage, she doesn't know where to start with the unpacking. Darren's the only Buttars brother who isn't married, and he wants to make Island Park his permanent home—with Farrah. Can they find their way through the heartache to achieve a happily-ever-after together?

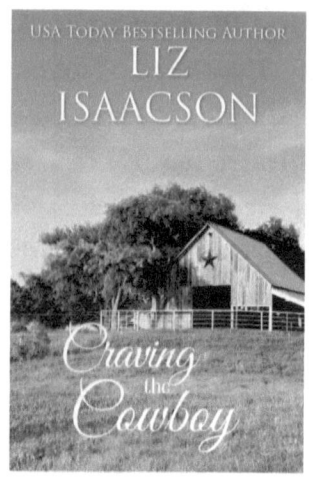

Craving the Cowboy (Book 1): Dwayne Carver is set to inherit his family's ranch in the heart of Texas Hill Country, and in order to keep up with his ranch duties and fulfill his dreams of owning a horse farm, he hires top trainer Felicity Lightburne. They get along great, and she can envision herself on this new farm—at least until her mother falls ill and she has to return to help her. Can Dwayne and Felicity work through their differences to find their happily-ever-after?

Charming the Cowboy (Book 2): Third grade teacher Heather Carver has had her eye on Levi Rhodes for a couple of years now, but he seems to be blind to her attempts to charm him. When she breaks her arm while on his horse ranch, Heather infiltrates Levi's life in ways he's never thought of, and his strict anti-female stance slips. Will Heather heal his emotional scars and he care for her physical ones so they can have a real relationship?

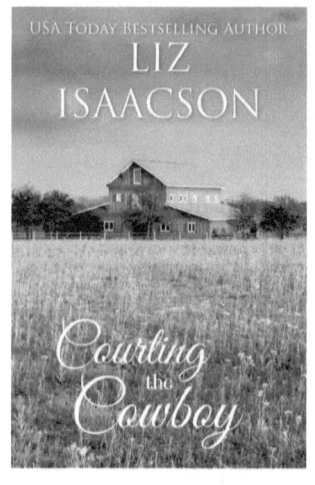

Courting the Cowboy (Book 3): Frustrated with the cowboy-only dating scene in Grape Seed Falls, May Sotheby joins TexasFaithful.com, hoping to find her soul mate without having to relocate--or deal with cowboy hats and boots. She has no idea that Kurt Pemberton, foreman at Grape Seed Ranch, is the man she starts communicating with... Will May be able to follow her heart and get Kurt to forgive her so they can be together?

Claiming the Cowboy, Royal Brothers Book 1 (Grape Seed Falls Romance Book 4): Unwilling to be tied down, farrier Robin Cook has managed to pack her entire life into a two-hundred-and-eighty square-foot house, and that includes her Yorkie. Cowboy and co-foreman, Shane Royal has had his heart set on Robin for three years, even though she flat-out turned him down the last time he asked her to dinner. But she's back at Grape Seed Ranch for five weeks as she works her horse-shoeing magic, and he's still interested, despite a bitter life lesson that left a bad taste for marriage in his mouth.

Robin's interested in him too. But can she find room for Shane in her tiny house--and can he take a chance on her with his tired heart?

Catching the Cowboy, Royal Brothers Book 2 (Grape Seed Falls Romance Book 5): Dylan Royal is good at two things: whistling and caring for cattle. When his cows are being attacked by an unknown wild animal, he calls Texas Parks & Wildlife for help. He wasn't expecting a beautiful mammologist to show up, all flirty and fun and everything Dylan didn't know he wanted in his life.

Hazel Brewster has gone on more first dates than anyone in Grape Seed Falls, and she thinks maybe Dylan deserves a second... Can they find their way through wild animals, huge life changes, and their emotional pasts to find their forever future?

Cheering the Cowboy, Royal Brothers Book 3 (Grape Seed Falls Romance Book 6): Austin Royal loves his life on his new ranch with his brothers. But he doesn't love that Shayleigh Hatch came with the property, nor that he has to take the blame for the fact that he now owns her childhood ranch. They rarely have a conversation that doesn't leave him furious and frustrated--and yet he's still attracted to Shay in a strange, new way.

Shay inexplicably likes him too, which utterly confuses and angers her. As they work to make this Christmas the best the Triple Towers Ranch has ever seen, can they also navigate through their rocky relationship to smoother waters?

Praise for Liz Isaacson

Choosing the Cowboy (Book 7): With financial trouble and personal issues around every corner, can Maggie Duffin and Chase Carver rely on their faith to find their happily-ever-after?

A spinoff from the #1 bestselling Three Rivers Ranch Romance novels, also by USA Today bestselling author Liz Isaacson.

Books in the Horseshoe Home Ranch
Romance Series:

The Redesigned Ranch (Book 1): Jace Lovell only has one thing left after his fiancé abandons him at the altar: his job at Horseshoe Home Ranch. Belle Edmunds is back in Gold Valley and she's desperate to build a portfolio that she can use to start her own firm in Montana. Jace isn't anywhere near forgiving his fiancé, and he's not sure he's ready for a new relationship with someone as fiery and beautiful as Belle. Can she employ her patience while he figures out how to forgive so they can find their own brand of happily-ever-after?

The Snowstorm in Gold Valley (Book 2): Professional snowboarder Sterling Maughan has sequestered himself in his family's cabin in the exclusive mountain community above Gold Valley, Montana after a devastating fall that ended his career. Norah Watson cleans Sterling's cabin and the more time they spend together, the more Sterling is interested in all things Norah. As his body heals, so does his faith. Will Norah be able to trust Sterling so they can have a chance at true love?

The Cabin on Bear Mountain (Book 3): Landon Edmunds has been a cowboy his whole life. An accident five years ago ended his successful rodeo career, and now he's looking to start a horse ranch-- and he's looking outside of Montana. Which would be great if God hadn't brought Megan Palmer back to Gold Valley right when Landon is looking to leave. Megan and Landon work together well, and as sparks fly, she's sure God brought her back to Gold Valley so she could find her happily ever after. Through serious discussion and prayer, can Landon and Megan find their future together?

Be sure to check out the spinoff series, the Brush Creek Brides romances after you read FALLING FOR HIS BEST FRIEND. Start with A WEDDING FOR THE WIDOWER.

The Cowboy at the Creek (Book 4): Twelve years ago, Owen Carr left Gold Valley—and his long-time girlfriend—in favor of a country music career in Nashville. Married and divorced, Natalie teaches ballet at the dance studio in Gold Valley, but she never auditioned for the professional company the way she dreamed of doing. With Owen back, she realizes all the opportunities she missed out on when he left all those years ago—including a future with him. Can they mend broken bridges in order to have a second chance at love?

The Wedding in the Winter (Book 5): Caleb Chamberlain has spent the last five years recovering from a horrible breakup, his alcoholism that stemmed from it, and the car accident that left him hospitalized. He's finally on the right track in his life—until Holly Gray, his twin brother's ex-fiance mistakes him for Nathan.

Holly's back in Gold Valley to get the required veterinarian hours to apply for her graduate program. When the herd at Horseshoe Home comes down with pneumonia, Caleb and Holly are forced to work together in close quarters. Holly's over Nathan, but she hasn't forgiven him—or the woman she believes broke up their relationship. Can Caleb and Holly navigate such a rough past to find their happily-ever-after?

The Long Way Home (Book 6): Ty Barker has been dancing through the last thirty years of his life--and he's suddenly realized he's alone. River Lee Whitely is back in Gold Valley with her two little girls after a divorce that's left deep scars. She has a job at Silver Creek that requires her to be able to ride a horse, and she nearly tramples Ty at her first lesson. That's just fine by him, because River Lee is the girl Ty has never gotten over. Ty realizes River Lee needs time to settle into her new job, her new home, her new life as a single parent, but going slow has never been his style. But for River Lee, can Ty take the necessary steps to keep her in his life?

Christmas at the Ranch (Book 7): Archer Bailey has already lost one job to Emersyn Enders, so he deliberately doesn't tell her about the cowhand job up at Horseshoe Home Ranch. Emery's temporary job is ending, but her obligations to her physically disabled sister aren't. As Archer and Emery work together, its clear that the sparks flying between them aren't all from their friendly competition over a job. Will Emery and Archer be able to navigate the ranch, their close quarters, and their individual circumstances to find love this holiday season?

The Love of a Cowboy (Book 8): Cowboy Elliott Hawthorne has just lost his best friend and cabin mate to the worst thing imaginable—marriage. When his brother calls about an accident with their father, Elliott rushes down to Gold Valley from the ranch only to be met with the most beautiful woman he's ever seen. His father's new physical therapist, London Marsh, likes the handsome face and gentle spirit she sees in Elliott too. Can Elliott and London navigate difficult family situations to find a happily-ever-after?

Books in the Brush Creek Brides Romance
Series:

Brush Creek Cowboy: Brush Creek Cowboys Romance (Book 1): Former rodeo champion and cowboy Walker Thompson trains horses at Brush Creek Horse Ranch, where he lives a simple life in his cabin with his ten-year-old son. A widower of six years, he's worked with Tess Wagner, a widow who came to Brush Creek to escape the turmoil of her life to give her seven-year-old son a slower pace of life. But Tess's breast cancer is back...

Walker will have to decide if he'd rather spend even a short time with Tess than not have her in his life at all. Tess wants to feel God's love and power, but can she discover and accept God's will in order to find her happy ending?

The Cowboy's Challenge: Brush Creek Brides Romance (Book 2): Cowboy and professional roper Justin Jackman has found solitude at Brush Creek Horse Ranch, preferring his time with the animals he trains over dating. With two failed engagements in his past, he's not really interested in getting his heart stomped on again. But when

flirty and fun Renee Martin picks him up at a church ice cream bar--on a bet, no less--he finds himself more than just a little interested. His Gen-X attitudes are attractive to her; her Millennial behaviors drive him nuts. Can Justin look past their differences and take a chance on another engagement?

A Cowboy Proposal: Brush Creek Brides Romance (Book 3): Ted Caldwell has been a retired bronc rider for years, and he thought he was perfectly happy training horses to buck at Brush Creek Ranch. He was wrong. When he meets April Nox, who comes to the ranch to hide her pregnancy from all her friends back in Jackson Hole, Ted realizes he has a huge family-shaped hole in his life. April is embarrassed, heartbroken, and trying to find her extinguished faith. She's never ridden a horse and wants nothing to do with a cowboy ever again. Can Ted and April create a family of happiness and love from a tragedy?

A New Family for the Cowboy: Brush Creek Brides Romance (Book 4): Blake Gibbons oversees all the agriculture at Brush Creek Horse Ranch, sometimes moonlighting as a general contractor. When he meets Erin Shields, new in town, at her aunt's bakery, he's instantly smitten. Erin moved to Brush Creek after a divorce that left  her penniless, homeless, and a single mother of three children under age eight. She's nowhere near ready to start dating again, but the longer Blake hangs around the bakery, the more she starts to like him. Can Blake and Erin find a way to blend their lifestyles and become a family?

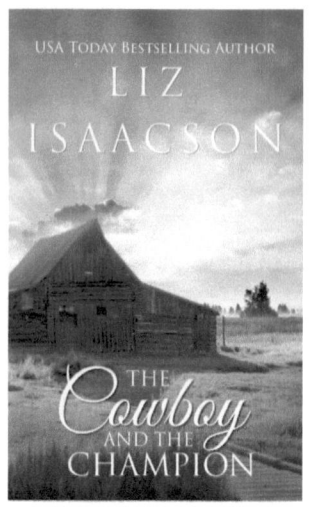

The Cowboy and the Champion: Brush Creek Brides Romance (Book 5): Emmett Graves has always had a positive outlook on life. He adores training horses to become barrel racing champions during the day and cuddling with his cat at night. Fresh off her professional rodeo retirement, Molly Brady comes to Brush Creek Horse Ranch as Emmett's protege. He's not thrilled, and she's allergic to cats. Oh, and she'd like to stay cowboy-free, thank you very much. But Emmett's about as cowboy as they come.... Can Emmett and Molly work together without falling in love?

Schooled by the Cowboy: Brush Creek Brides Romance (Book 6): Grant Ford spends his days training cattle—when he's not camped out at the elementary school hoping to catch a glimpse of his ex-girlfriend. When principal Shannon Sharpe confronts him and asks him to stay away from the school, the spark between them is instant and hot. Shan-

non's expecting a transfer very soon, but she also needs a summer outdoor coordinator—and Grant fits the bill. Just because he's handsome and everything Shannon's ever wanted in a cowboy husband means nothing. Will Grant and Shannon be able to survive the summer or will the Utah heat be too much for them to handle?

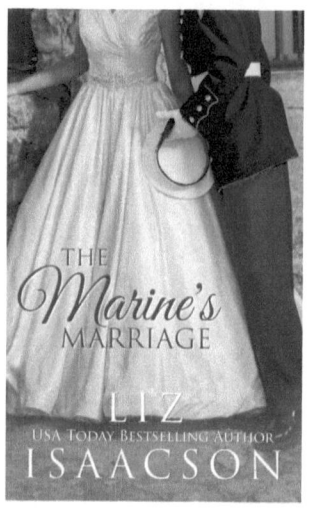

The Marine's Marriage: A Fuller Family Novel - Brush Creek Brides Romance (Book 1): Tate Benson can't believe he's come to Nowhere, Utah, to fix up a house that hasn't been inhabited in years. But he has. Because he's retired from the Marines and looking to start a life as a police officer in small-town Brush Creek. Wren Fuller has her hands full most days running her family's company. When Tate calls and demands a maid for that morning, she decides to have the calls forwarded to her cell and go help him out. She didn't know he was moving in next door, and she's completely unprepared for his handsomeness, his kind heart, and his wounded soul.Can Tate and Wren weather a relationship when they're also next-door neighbors?

The Firefighter's Fiancé: A Fuller Family Novel - Brush Creek Brides Romance (Book 2): Cora Wesley comes to Brush Creek, hoping to get some in-the-wild firefighting training as she prepares to put in her application to be a hotshot. When she meets Brennan Fuller, the spark between them is hot and instant. As they get to know  each other, her deadline is constantly looming over them, and Brennan starts to wonder if he can break ranks in the family business. He's okay mowing lawns and hanging out with his brothers, but he dreams of being able to go to college and become a landscape architect, but he's just not sure it can be done. Will Cora and Brennan be able to endure their trials to find true love?

The Trooper's Treasure: A Fuller Family Novel - Brush Creek Brides Romance (Book 3): Dawn Fuller has made some mistakes in her life, and she's not proud of the way McDermott Boyd found her off the road one day last year. She's spent a hard year wrestling with her choices and trying to fix them, glad for McDermott's acceptance and friendship. He lost his wife years ago, done his best with his daughter, and now he's ready to move on. Can McDermott help Dawn find a way past her former mistakes and down a path that leads to love, family, and happiness?

The Detective's Date: A Fuller Family Novel - Brush Creek Brides Romance (Book 4): Dahlia Reid is one of the best detectives Brush Creek and the surrounding towns has ever had. She's given up on the idea of marriage—and pleasing her mother—and has dedicated herself fully to her job. Which is great, since one of the most perplexing

cases of her career has come to town. Kyler Fuller thinks he's finally ready to move past the woman who ghosted him years ago. He's cut his hair, and he's ready to start dating. Too bad every woman he's been out with is about as interesting as a lamppost—until Dahlia. He finds her beautiful, her quick wit a breath of fresh air, and her intelligence sexy. Can Kyler and Dahlia use their faith to find a way through the obstacles threatening to keep them apart?

The Paramedic's Partner: A Fuller Family Novel - Brush Creek Brides Romance (Book 5): Jazzy Fuller has always been overshadowed by her prettier, more popular twin, Fabiana. Fabi meets paramedic Max Robinson at the park and sets a date with him only to come down with the flu. So she convinces Jazzy to cut her hair and take her place on the date. And the spark between Jazzy and Max is hot and instant...if only he knew she wasn't her sister, Fabi.

Max drives the ambulance for the town of Brush Creek with is partner Ed Moon, and neither of them have been all that lucky in love. Until Max suggests to who he thinks is Fabi that they should double with Ed and Jazzy. They do, and Fabi is smitten with the steady, strong Ed Moon. As each twin falls further and further in love with their respective paramedic, it becomes obvious they'll need to come clean about the switcheroo sooner rather than later...or risk losing their hearts.

The Chief's Catch: A Fuller Family Novel - Brush Creek Brides Romance (Book 6): Berlin Fuller has struck out with the dating scene in Brush Creek more times than she cares to admit. When she makes a deal with her friends that they can choose the next man she goes out with, she didn't dream they'd pick surly Cole Fairbanks, the new Chief of Police.

His friends call him the Beast and challenge him to complete ten dates that summer or give up his bonus check. When Berlin approaches him, stuttering about the deal with her friends and claiming they don't actually have to go out, he's intrigued. As the summer passes, Cole finds himself burning both ends of the candle to keep up with his job and his new relationship. When he unleashes the Beast one time too many, Berlin will have to decide if she can tame him or if she should walk away.

About Liz

Liz Isaacson writes inspirational romance, usually set in Texas, or Montana, or anywhere else horses and cowboys exist. She lives in Utah, where she writes full-time, walks her two dogs daily, and eats a lot of peanut butter M&Ms while writing. Find her on her website at lizisaacson.com.

www.ingramcontent.com/pod-product-compliance
Lightning Source LLC
Chambersburg PA
CBHW020717130726
47899CB00011B/327